✦✦✦✦✦✦✦✦✦✦✦✦✦

FINAL
PROOF

✦✦✦✦✦✦✦✦✦✦✦✦✦

A JOAN KAHN BOOK

FINAL PROOF

BY

MARIE R. RENO

HARPER & ROW, PUBLISHERS
New York, Hagerstown,
San Francisco, London

A HARPER NOVEL OF SUSPENSE

FINAL PROOF. Copyright © 1976 by Marie R. Reno. All rights reserved. Printed in the United States of America. No part of this book may be used or reproduced in any manner whatsoever without written permission except in the case of brief quotations embodied in critical articles and reviews: For information address Harper & Row, Publishers, Inc., 10 East 53rd Street, New York, N.Y. 10022. Published simultaneously in Canada by Fitzhenry & Whiteside Limited, Toronto.

FIRST EDITION

Designed by Janice Willcocks Stern

Library of Congress Cataloging in Publication Data

Reno, Marie, R.
  Final proof.
  I. Title.
PZ4.R417Fi [PS3568.E65]   813'.5'4   75–30355
ISBN 0–06–013564–6

---

76 77 78 79 10 9 8 7 6 5 4 3 2 1

1

Marcia Richardson was found slumped over a set of galley proofs on a Tuesday morning in mid-July. She had been dead at least twelve hours, the police estimated, shot twice through the head at close range by a .22 revolver. Although her fingers had been wrapped around the gun in a clumsy attempt to make the death look like suicide, there was little doubt that she had been murdered. Who ever heard of a suicide who pulled the trigger twice?

Now that Marcia is dead and buried, everybody carries on as if she had been a saint. I think she would have been embarrassed by so much extravagant praise. And by so much talk, too, she was a very private person. She was my friend—and my boss—and I thought she did a first-class job running the Readers' Circle Book Club. That's the third of the big three in publishing circles: Book-of-the-Month Club, Literary Guild, and Readers' Circle. I'm an associate editor of RC, one of nine reading for the club, but actually I spend half my time choosing books for MSI—that's Mystery, Suspense, and Intrigue, a smaller club that's part of the general book-club division. (We are all a part of the Berwyn Publishing Company, which in turn is part of the multi-national conglomerate Phoenix Industries.)

Anyway, I was perfectly happy being editor of MSI, and Marcia let me do pretty much as I pleased with the club. It was making money, always a happy state of affairs, and I had no more than the usual amount of trouble with the Harvard Business School types who run around meddling with a going operation.

My name, by the way, is Karen Lindstrom, I'm twenty-eight years old, and I came to New York six years ago from Neenah, Wisconsin, as soon as I finished college and saved enough money to get away. My mother still thinks I should have stayed home and married the boy next door, but I always thought Gary was pretty boring, if you want to know the truth, even if he was nice-looking and never went through that pimply, awkward stage. Anyway, he's married to Joanie Peterson now, and you can't go home again.

Marcia's murder really shook up my parents, though, and they started in all over again about how dangerous it is to be living in New York.

I don't really mean to be flippant about Marcia's death. It was terrible and shocking, and in some ways I suppose I'll never get over it. But the truth is that I just don't know how to talk about death, and I never know what to say at funerals or what to write in sympathy letters. I said that to Lieutenant Jack Morrison the first day I met him —he was one of the detectives on the case, the first New York City cop I ever met—and he said most people are the same way. The first wake he ever went to, when he was new on the force, he had never heard so many crazy jokes or seen so much Scotch in one place. He wound up staying all night and having a wonderful time. Of course he hadn't really known the cop who had been killed.

But I was going to tell you about Marcia. When she wasn't in her office by ten o'clock that Tuesday (we keep lax hours in publishing, but Marcia was never later than 9:30), Wendy Lyle, her secretary, phoned her at home to see if there was any problem. Marcia was divorced and had two children, both boys, but they were away at camp for the month of July, so Marcia was alone. When there was no answer, Wendy assumed she was on her way, but twenty minutes later she was getting worried; it doesn't take all that long to get from West End Avenue to Rockefeller Center. When another phone call failed to get an answer, Wendy somehow tracked down the building superintendent and persuaded him to check out Marcia's apartment. He's the one who found the body and called the police. He called Wendy, too, and she went into hysterics. That's the first time I ever saw that happen, and it's scary. We called the nurse from the clinic, and she took Wendy away and gave her a sedative or something.

Well, of course the office was in an uproar, and all we did was stand around in little groups and speculate about who could have done it and what the police would say when they came. Joe Blackwell, the managing editor and Marcia's second in command, thought to call George Griffith, the president of the division, so the news spread to the marketing side, and pretty soon we had all the business people cluttering up our offices, too.

In the midst of this commotion, my telephone rang. It was somebody from Random House, asking about my decision on a mystery. I explained about Marcia's murder, and then I took a phone call from Viking and went through it all again. Jerry Goulden, the Sports Book Club editor, who occupies the office next to mine, was getting phone calls, too, and I realized the news would be all over the publishing world before the police ever got to us.

A *New York Times* reporter was on the phone to Joe Blackwell, checking out the story, just as the cops arrived. It's really true when they call us a communications industry.

It was almost noon by then, and most of us had lunch dates, but the police didn't want anybody to leave until they'd had a chance to talk to us individually. Two of the editors made a big production out of canceling reservations at the Italian Pavilion and Gloucester House and ordering sandwiches sent up instead, but I wasn't hungry. Anyway, I was secretly rather glad to be present at a real murder investigation. After all those Agatha Christies and Rex Stouts, I could see the real thing.

Actually, I didn't see much of anything. The cops had taken over Marcia's office, and they called in all of us, one by one, starting with the president of the division, George Griffith. I couldn't imagine that George knew *any*thing. Wendy was interviewed, too; she had calmed down by then, but she was sobbing again when she left Marcia's office.

It didn't really take them all that long, though they kept Joe Blackwell in there half an hour. I hung back on purpose, hoping to be the last one so that I could find out if they had learned anything in all the earlier interviews.

All three cops looked bored by the time they got around to me, and it was after 1:30 by then and they were hungry. They gave me some formula line about how we should all cooperate, and they asked if I'd be willing to answer questions. And of course I certainly was. One of them—it turned out to be Lieutenant Jack Morrison—appeared inter-

3

ested in the fact that I was editor of MSI, and he went so far as to ask what the difference was between mystery, suspense, and intrigue. I was explaining the technicalities of what we call police procedurals when the second cop told him to cut that shit and get on with the case.

Lieutenant Morrison gave him a dirty look, and I tried to pretend I hadn't heard, but after all I went to college in the 1960s and my vocabulary stretched out in all directions. Anyway, we got back to the case, and they all paid attention when I said I had tried to phone Marcia at ten o'clock the night before and there had been no answer. It was particularly significant because I had tried to reach her earlier, about nine, and the line had been busy. I was calling to say that the suspense novel I was reading was wonderful and I was going to buy it for MSI and she ought to consider it for Readers' Circle, too, but they didn't care about that. They took me through the times of the phone calls over and over again, though, and asked me how I could be sure it was about nine the first time. The symphony was just going off on WQXR and I got up to shut off the commercial. That's how I knew it was almost nine. And then I read some of *New York* Magazine, and at 9:30 I turned on my TV set and decided to catch a rerun of *Maude.* When it was over, I called her. That's how I knew it was ten o'clock. They had their tape recorder spinning through all of this, but Lieutenant Morrison made notes anyway.

By the time they were finished with that, the office was deserted (I don't think there had been an official announcement about taking the rest of the day off, but we all did anyway).

The three of them had a hurried discussion of something or other, and then Lieutenant Morrison invited me to lunch, under the umbrellas in Rockefeller Center. I asked if it was on his expense account and if I would be a material witness, but he just laughed. It occurred to me that maybe I could use *my* expense account (shouldn't the MSI editor do some basic research with real cops?), but I didn't mention that.

It was one of those rare days in July when the sunlight sparkled, the temperature was somewhere in the seventies, and the humidity was so low that nobody mentioned it. The waiter seated us immediately, right beside the gilded Prometheus, and then he hovered over

4

us attentively—too attentively, I thought. I wondered if he knew I was with a policeman.

It turned out that Lieutenant Morrison wanted a complete run-down on everybody in the office and everybody in publishing and everything I knew about Marcia from the time I first met her. But at least he began by explaining something about the case. He had arrived on the scene before eleven, had detained the super for questioning, and was making arrangements for photographs and all those routine things when the phone rang and it was *The New York Times*. That call was followed almost immediately by one from the *Village Voice*, of all things. (I knew that our Crafts Club editor was living with a reporter on the staff, but I didn't interrupt at that point.)

Lieutenant Morrison realized that the case was going to make headlines and he had better call his captain, Frank Reilly, and explain the set-up. The last thing he wanted was another Wylie-Hoffert case. That was the murder of two New York career girls, and the police went after the wrong man. It was all kind of embarrassing. Not to mention being pretty dreadful for the guy in jail, too.

"I read about that," I said. "Wasn't there some question about whether the next man convicted was really guilty, too? It seems to me there was a book about it."

"People write too many books," Lieutenant Morrison said, and I couldn't help agreeing with him.

So, the captain arrived, with a deputy chief inspector, and they took over the case. After a hasty survey of the scene, the captain said that Morrison had better hustle down to Marcia's office and see if he could shut us all up. Which was impossible, of course. Anyway, Lieutenant Morrison assumed that the investigation was going on back in the apartment building, and Frank Reilly had probably notified Marcia's ex-husband by now and maybe asked him to call the two boys at camp. Lieutenant Morrison asked me about the rest of the family, but I had never met them. Her mother was a widow, living in Philadelphia, I thought, and there was a married brother up in Connecticut somewhere. The police would find an address book, probably, or check out the information with Marcia's ex-husband, Harry.

"Was she on good terms with Harry?" Lieutenant Morrison asked.

"Off and on," I said. "They were divorced two years ago, and she got the co-op apartment in town and he kept the fishing shack up in the Berkshires. He usually takes the boys there in August, but she has custody the rest of the year. And she gets child support, I think, but no alimony."

"Did they fight about money?"

"Marcia doesn't fight. Didn't fight," I amended. "She just said what she was going to do, or what she thought you ought to do. And if you disagreed, she'd listen for the reason. Sometimes she even changed her mind and agreed with you. But if she thought she was right, she went straight ahead."

"I don't get it. Suppose she said 'I want a thousand a month for the kids,' and he said 'I'll give you five hundred,' then what?"

"She knew his financial situation better than he did. If she said a thousand a month or whatever, and he said no, she probably turned the whole thing over to her lawyer. When Harry was being 'difficult,' as she called it, she just wouldn't talk to him when he called."

"Did he call a lot?"

"I think so, but her secretary would know, at least about the office calls. Harry took an apartment just a few blocks away from the boys' school—they're at Trinity, I think—and he saw them a couple of times a week, usually took them out to dinner on Thursdays."

"Did you know him at all? What kind of man is he?"

"I met him a couple of times. He's a dentist. I don't know. What can you say about a dentist? I didn't go to him. I thought about showing him my gold inlays when we were first introduced (they cost me a lot of money), but I didn't, of course."

Lieutenant Morrison gave me a withering glance, but I don't wither easily.

"Why did you ask me all those questions about telephoning Marcia last night? How could you pin down the time of her death before the medical examiner saw her?"

"We didn't 'pin down the time of her death' yet. But it looked obvious to us that she had been killed last night. Her body was cold, her bed hadn't been slept in, and she was wearing street clothes. On the surface, at any rate, it looked as if she had been sitting at her desk in the living room, reading. The dishes were clean in the dishwasher.

She probably had had dinner—the medical examiner will tell us about that—and she hadn't gotten ready for bed yet. I understand from all of you that she was in the office yesterday, left about five forty-five, and took a taxi home." He consulted his notes. "The managing editor, Joe Blackwell, saw her getting into a cab, and he just assumed she was going home. But all that will be checked out. They've got a doorman in that building where she lives. Maybe he'll remember."

"Maybe. Marcia complained that he was a drunk. I wouldn't put much faith in him. She felt a little uneasy in that building after the elevators were converted to manual operation. Anybody could slip in past the doorman and go right up. She saw a couple of teen-age kids running down the firestairs last week, and she later learned that they had forced the door in the apartment right over hers. I think they were scared off without getting anything, though—the tenant came back from walking his dog and they ran out the service door."

Lieutenant Morrison made some more notes. He wasn't making much progress with his hamburger, I noticed, and I was just picking at my fruit salad. I had stopped altogether when he made that remark about the medical examiner determining whether Marcia had had dinner last night.

"Do you know if she had a gun?" he asked.

"Why, yes, she did. I forgot about that. I think she kept it in the bedroom, in a drawer in her night table. I was kind of surprised when she told me about that. I think she got it after she and Harry split up."

"You mean she was afraid of him?"

"Oh, no. Not Harry. It was just the idea of being there by herself. New York gets to some people. She had a full-time housekeeper when the boys were smaller, but now there's just a maid who comes in the afternoons."

"What kind of gun was it?"

"I don't know. I never saw it."

"But you said she kept it in her night table."

"Yes, she told me that. We were sitting around at lunch one day, four or five of us, and we got to talking about what you would do if you got home and found a burglar in your apartment. I said I'd sneak away and hope I hadn't disturbed him; then I'd head for the nearest telephone and call the police."

"That's reasonably sensible."

"Marcia said she would, too, but she said it would be more complicated if she thought the boys were there with the burglar. Anyway, that's when she told us she had a gun. Maybe she was right, too—she just wasn't able to get to the bedroom to find it."

"But maybe her visitor did."

"What do you mean?"

"There was no gun in the night table, though the drawer was open and we could see where it had been kept. I think she was killed with her own twenty-two. I was just starting a search through her papers, to see if she had registered it, when Frank arrived."

"Frank?"

"Frank Reilly. I told you. Captain Reilly. He's probably checked out the registration by now."

"Yes, probably." I took another sip of coffee and stared at him. He was certainly different from what I expected cops to be like, and I told him so.

"That's what Frank says, too. I always tell him it's because I majored in psychology."

"You didn't!"

"Sure. Queens College, class of '65."

"Why did you ever become a cop?"

"Well, basically because I didn't want to go to Vietnam. I couldn't see any point in slogging around in those rice paddies over there. I knew I'd be losing my student deferment, and there was a rumor going around that policemen were exempt from the draft, and one thing led to another. The mayor had a big campaign on then to change the image of the cops, and there was a recruiting drive at a lot of colleges. I think they were after Ivy League types, but they got a little bit of everything. Sort of a greening of the police force."

"Did it work?"

"Well, maybe a little bit around the edges. More likely it was a bluing of all the green recruits. Some of us turned out a rather nice shade of aquamarine, I think."

"Is that why you told me so much about the case? Because you're practicing psychology?"

"Partly. Anyway, I don't think I'm giving away state secrets. I don't think I've told you anything you won't be able to read in the *Times* or the *Daily News* tomorrow." He consulted his watch. "I have another half hour before I call in. Let's have some ice cream."

The waiter appeared immediately—civilians never get that kind of service.

"Let's get back to the case. You didn't know the former husband very well. Do you know if he had a girl friend? Was he thinking about marrying again?"

"You're really interested in him, aren't you?"

"I'm interested in anything you can tell me about anybody who knew Marcia. So, did Harry have a girl friend?"

"I don't really know." There was something rattling around in the back of my head, something Marcia had told me. And then I remembered. "Marcia said something, something about his newfound interest in home economics and a little woman who would stay home and bake bread. It was a very strange thing for Marcia to say. She didn't go around making catty remarks about people."

"You don't know what she meant by that?"

"No." I shook my head. The waiter arrived with the ice cream and more coffee, and we were temporarily distracted.

Lieutenant Morrison put down his pen to add cream to his coffee. He has nice hands. No rings.

"What about Marcia?" he began again.

"What about her?"

"Any men in her life now? Any jealous boy friends hanging around?"

"You really have to know all this? The poor woman is dead, and you have to go probing around in her life like this?"

"Yes. I'm sorry. In a case like this, a murder victim loses all privacy. Any boy friends?"

"Well, there's Marty Bayliss, but I don't think he counts. Marty is . . . just sort of a convenient escort. He's a free-lance writer, does articles and reviews."

"He's queer?"

"Yes, I think so."

"Anybody else?"

"I don't really know. That lawyer who handled her divorce. I think

9

she saw him once in a while. I don't know his name. I wasn't Marcia's best friend, you know. I mean, I suppose I was as close to her as anybody in the office, but that doesn't mean she told me all the intimate details of her personal life."

"I see. Do you know who might know?"

"I'm not sure. Maybe Meredith Baker. She's an agent; she was Marcia's agent and knew her for a long time. Marcia used to do quite a lot of writing, short stories, mostly, when the boys were very young and she was at home with them. I didn't know her then, of course. I've only been with RC for three years."

"OK. Let's talk about the office. How did she get along with everybody? Anybody hate her? Want her out of the way?"

"Of course not! We liked her. And anyway, what kind of people do you think we are? We don't go around killing each other."

"Somebody killed Marcia."

"I know. But it's still so unreal. I can't imagine anybody at the office picking up a gun and aiming it at her."

"What about this managing editor?" He riffled through his notes. "Joe Blackwell. Will he get her job now? Is he very ambitious? Does he need money? Did he mind working for a woman?"

I shook my head in disbelief. "Joe is as gentle and nice a guy as you can imagine. How can you possibly suspect him?"

"I don't necessarily suspect him. I'm just asking questions. He is somebody who might benefit from her death. *I* don't know. Don't jump to conclusions. I asked him about you, after all."

"You did? You hadn't even met me at that point."

"I got a list of everybody on the staff when I first arrived. I asked who knew Marcia best, and it was a toss-up between you and Blackwell. So I asked him about you, and now I'm asking you about him."

"Oh. Oh, that's why I'm here. You just wanted to ask me a lot of questions."

"Well, sure. I told you that right at the beginning. What did you think? That I just invited you to lunch because you're pretty? Or maybe you thought you could help solve the case because you've read so much mystery, suspense, and intrigue." He started to laugh, because of course he had read my mind completely. Not that I really believed I *could* solve the case, you understand, but it had crossed my mind.

I struggled for a dignified reply to put him in his place, but it was no use, and I blushed and giggled, which is something I hadn't planned to do at all.

"All right, you win." He reached over and covered my right hand with his. "I also asked you out to lunch because you're pretty. Now let's get back to Joe Blackwell. Will he get Marcia's job?" He was going right on as though nothing had happened. His hand was right back there on his notebook, and he was waiting expectantly for an answer.

"Joe Blackwell," I began. "I don't know if he'll get Marcia's job or if they'll bring in somebody from the outside. Are you married?"

"Divorced," he said briefly. "Will Blackwell be disappointed if he doesn't get it?"

"I suppose so. Wouldn't you be? What was your wife like?"

He looked at me, and then he looked at his watch, and then he stood up. "I have to call in. I guess you'd better wait. This is going to take longer than I thought."

It was almost three when he got back, and the sun had shifted and I was starting to get hot. He paid off the waiter and stood looking at me speculatively for a minute. "Where do you live?"

"East Eighty-seventh Street, just off York. Where do you live?"

"Jackson Heights. I'll run you home."

"Oh, that's all right. Really. I thought I'd just walk over to Bloomingdale's and then get a bus."

"Look, Miss Lindstrom, I'm not doing you any favors. I still have questions to ask you. I can take you to the station house, or we can go on sitting here, even though the temperature has shot up five degrees in the last hour, or you can hop in the car and maybe we can finish up on the drive home."

He couldn't make notes while he was driving, so he wound up answering *my* questions most of the time. I found out that he had been married for five years and divorced for a year and a half. No children. His wife had studied interior design and was working for some decorator up in Westchester. Living with him, too, for all he knew.

11

"We believe in too many stereotypes," he said, pulling up to the curb in front of my apartment house. "I thought interior decorating was full of queers. And then she walked out on me for her boss." He shrugged.

I got out of the car, and he did, too.

"I thought we were all finished," I said.

"Almost. Another ten minutes. Aren't you going to ask me in?"

"But what about the car, in a no-parking zone?"

"What about it?"

It seemed to be a rhetorical question.

I live on the third floor of a converted brownstone, rather nice, really, if you don't mind all the stairs. The Salvation Army furniture is gradually being retired in favor of Danish modern, and the living room is practically finished, now that my rya rug has finally been delivered.

Lieutenant Morrison took it all in with a glance, spotted the telephone in the bedroom, and went in and picked it up—to see if there was a dial tone, I guess.

"You couldn't have dialed the wrong number last night, could you, when you were trying to reach Marcia?"

"I could have, I suppose, but I don't think so."

"Did you make any other calls? Or get any?"

"I don't remember making any. But my parents called from Wisconsin."

"Good. There'll be a record of that. When?"

"Let me think. I had just finished the dishes, and Walter Cronkite was signing off. That would be seven thirty."

"Don't you ever look at a clock? Do you time everything by what's on the radio or television? Never mind. What's that phone number in Wisconsin?"

I gave it to him, but a funny little knot of fear was starting to form somewhere in the pit of my stomach, and I was finding it difficult to breathe. It was awfully hot, too, I suddenly realized, and I walked over to the air-conditioner in the window and turned it on.

He was still writing in that little notebook. "Did you see or talk to anybody else after you had that conversation with your parents?"

"No." My voice sounded funny, even to me, and Lieutenant Morrison looked at me sharply.

"What's the matter?"

"I'm frightened. You sound as if you really suspect me." My voice cracked then, and I started to cry. "You don't understand. I *liked* Marcia. I can still hardly believe she's dead. We were friends . . ." But I couldn't go on. I turned my back on him and stared blindly out the window. Eventually he came over and handed me a tissue and suggested that I have a drink of water and calm down. He seemed to be acutely embarrassed, and so was I.

"I didn't mean to upset you, Miss Lindstrom."

"I know. It just hit me all of a sudden. Marcia's dead, and it's murder, and somehow I'm right in the middle of it. It's not just another Agatha Christie."

"Yes. Death affects people in different ways." That's when he told me about going to his first wake. And staying all night because it was such a blast. By the time we got all that straightened out, we were on a first-name basis and I was in the kitchen pouring us each a glass of lemonade.

And then he got his notebook out again and we went through every single person on the editorial staff of RC.

He asked me who would get the managing editor's job if Joe Blackwell was promoted; and he asked me about what would happen to Marcia's secretary; and he found out the connection between Lucy Michaelson, the Crafts Club editor, and the reporter from the *Village Voice;* and he asked me if I wanted to be promoted to managing editor.

"Good grief, no. I'd have to work too hard. I'd be taking home manuscripts every night."

"You were reading something last night."

"Oh, maybe once a month I come across something I like so much that I take it home to finish right away. But that's quite exceptional. Usually it can wait until next day. Marcia was reading all the time, though, and Joe, too."

Jack leafed back through his notes. "She had a set of galleys on the desk: *Forbidden Passion* by Richmond Frazier."

"That's funny. I was first reader on that and thought it was terrible. Full of incest and really nasty sex scenes. Well, I suppose the publisher was pushing her and she thought she had to pay it some attention."

"Explain to me how all this works."

"Well, you see, publishers like to have their books chosen by a book club, and so do authors. It means more money, of course, but it also means that the book is likely to get more attention, particularly if it is taken by one of the majors, the Literary Guild or the Book-of-the-Month Club or Readers' Circle. The book will be appearing in ads, television is more likely to sign up the author for talk shows, the paperback houses are more likely to bid for the book. Everything sort of reinforces everything else."

"I see. So the book clubs look at what the reviewers are saying and check what is on the best-seller lists and decide to—"

"No, not at all. That would be too late. We get the books long before they are published, when they are still in manuscript or galley proof. This is July, and we're reading books that won't come out until December, January, February, spring."

"Then how do you decide what to take?"

"Basically, it's whether we like it or not. But there are other factors at work, too. We look at the track record of the author—if he has sold well before. Not just the best-seller lists but the sales in the clubs, too. We have computer print-outs on everything these days, and if we know the author is popular with book-club members, that's very important. And then we listen to what the publishers say, how enthusiastic they are in terms of big printings and advertising budgets and all that. And if the movies are interested, that might mean something. It all depends on the particular book. Actually, when you get right down to it, the book is what it all hangs on, and there's no way to program that exactly. If we like something a lot, we'll buy it, even if the publisher isn't pushing it like mad and the author is completely unknown. If a book like that makes it, a real sleeper, that's the most fun of all. It's like a discovery. I mean, it's easy and unremarkable to buy a big-name author and have a big success. It costs a lot of money to outbid the other clubs, and you might sweat out whether you're bidding too high, but you're dealing with the known. When Marcia buys a little book for RC that goes on to be a tremendous success,

14

that's when she has really accomplished something."

"And you don't think this one, this *Forbidden Passion*, is going to make it?"

"No. But I'm not exactly infallible. And maybe the publisher was bugging her about it. That can happen."

"Did it bother her when publishers bugged her? I mean, do they get really mad when you turn down their books?"

"They are disappointed, maybe. But that's part of the job. They'll be back the next day with something else. It's kind of a symbiotic relationship, and we all depend on each other. And sometimes they turn *us* down because they get a better offer from another book club."

"I see. And how does that make you feel?"

"Well, of course we hate to lose a book to the Guild or to Book-of-the-Month. But I wouldn't say it made us mad enough to go and kill somebody. There's always another book around, for heaven's sake."

"Just for the record, though, had Readers' Circle just bought a book that one of your rivals wanted?"

"God, you're persistent. Let me think. BOM just took the new Solzhenitsyn, and Guild . . . That's right. We outbid them on some new Watergate book that's supposed to be terrific. The definitive book on Nixon. I didn't read it, but Joe and Marcia said it was first-class."

"Good. Well, that about does it for now. I'll probably be back if I have more questions. And if you think of anything else I should know, call me." He wrote down his name and rank and telephone number and gave it to me.

"Thanks very much, Karen. You really have been helpful, and I'm sorry I upset you." He shook hands, very formally, and I saw him to the door.

I was feeling pretty strung out by then, and I collapsed on the couch for half an hour, trying to sort it all out in my mind. It had all been so unreal, starting with Wendy's hysteria on the phone. We had all been in shock those first few hours. I must have sounded like a real idiot at lunch, babbling away with Jack as if we had been on our first date or something. It hadn't really hit me at all at first, and I still wasn't sure of all the implications. Marcia was dead, and somebody had killed her. Maybe somebody I know. I got up and rechecked the door, to make sure it was double-locked, and I inspected the gate over the window leading to the fire escape. And then I remembered to turn on the radio for the news. I sat through an endless weather forecast and two commercials and a long bit about the scandal in the mental hospitals, and finally they came to the murder.

"Mrs. Marcia Richardson, editorial director of the Readers' Circle Book Club, was found dead in her apartment on West End Avenue this morning. The police said she had been shot twice through the head with her own twenty-two revolver. There was no sign of forced entry. The report from the medical examiner has not yet been released, but there was speculation that she had been dead at least twelve hours when the body was discovered. Captain Frank Reilly, who was interviewed at the scene, declined further comment, refusing even to say whether the death was murder or suicide.

"The body was discovered about ten thirty this morning by the building superintendent, Joseph Mercato. He had no doubt that it was murder. There was no suicide note, he said, and he couldn't believe anybody could shoot himself in the head twice."

Then there was something about an intensive investigation and a special phone number to call. I wrote it down, but it was different from the one Jack had given me.

The six-o'clock news on television was much the same. They flashed a picture of Marcia on the screen, the one that was distributed when she was named editorial director four years ago. Then there was a tape of the confusion outside her building when her body, completely shrouded by blankets, was loaded in an ambulance. The building super repeated his comments about the impossibility of suicide, and Captain Frank Reilly and a deputy chief inspector whose name I didn't catch steadily refused further comment. The anchorman read off the special telephone number to call and then turned his attention to a six-car collision on the West Side Highway.

I decided to call my parents in Wisconsin; I didn't think the murder would make the network news shows, but I wasn't sure. In any case, it was better for them to hear it directly from me.

My mother took it better than my father, strangely enough, though of course they both started in all over again about my coming home. I listened to all that for a while, and then I sidetracked my mother by asking her about Rob's wedding. Rob is my younger brother, and

16

he's getting married next month in Washington. My parents are coming east for the wedding, and they'll be in New York for a couple of days afterward. We had been through all that when they phoned me the night before, but I didn't mind talking about it again. It sounded so nice and normal. Then my father cut in (he was on the extension upstairs), and he said the call was costing me a lot of money and we should hang up and they'd call back the next day to see if the murderer had been caught. So I agreed to that and we all said good-by.

I prowled around the apartment for a while and ate a banana and listened to Walter Cronkite (nothing about the murder), but I couldn't settle down to anything, so I went up to the fourth floor and rang Elly's doorbell. Elly Crawford is kind of weird—she believes in astrology and yoga and ESP and flying saucers and the Bermuda Triangle and maybe even little green men—but she lives right in the building, and I depend on her to water my house plants and take care of my mail while I'm away, and I do the same for her. She came to New York wanting to be an actress, and she still haunts Off-Broadway and Off-Off-Broadway. Once she made a television commercial for dog food and collected residuals for a year. But mostly she signs up for part-time work at Olsten's and takes temporary jobs. This week she was filling in at some real-estate company.

Anyway, she had just finished painting her fingernails when I arrived, and she listened with flattering attention to my tale of murder.

"It's her husband," she said flatly. "Her ex-husband. He's got a double motive—he wants the children, and he's tired of paying out all that money every month. I bet he's got a girl friend, too, and she's forced him into it. Lady Macbeth. Maybe *she's* guilty, too."

"Oh, Elly!"

"Well, why not? He must have known about the gun. He certainly knew where she lived, and he could sneak in past the doorman. He could have phoned her at nine, when you were trying to reach her, and invited himself over. And when you called again, he was right in the middle of killing her. Maybe he took his girl friend along and she fired the gun once, too, so they would both be guilty. What do you think?"

"I don't know. It could have happened that way, maybe. But I've met Harry. He's not like that. He's a dentist, for heaven's sake."

"So? Dentists are human, too. They can stand the sight of blood. You should have seen me when I had my wisdom tooth pulled. Blood all over."

It was hot in Elly's apartment (she didn't have an air-conditioner), and I was suddenly feeling a little queasy.

"Are you all right?" Elly prided herself on her powers of observation; tuning in on the vibes, she said.

"I'm just sort of . . . restless. I want to forget about it for a few hours, I guess. Want to see a movie?"

She was agreeable, and there was a new Robert Redford picture playing on 86th Street. I was starved by the time it was over, so we stopped for a hamburger, and for a while everything seemed almost normal again.

2

I picked up both the *Times* and the *Daily News* on the way to work next morning. The *Daily News* had the story on page seven with a three-column picture of the body (covered up) being carried out to the ambulance. The *Times* had a one-column headline below the fold on page one, with a head shot of Marcia on the jump page, the same studio pose that had been on television the day before. Neither story had much new information. I learned that the doorman, José García, was new and he still didn't know all the tenants. That meant they had fired the drunk who had been there, I supposed. Would that make him a suspect? I knew Marcia had complained about him to the super. Tough luck about this José García, though. He wouldn't know a stranger from a tenant, and he probably had let anybody in.

There was a brief biography of Marcia, briefer in the *News* than in the *Times*, and a quote from our company president expressing shock and praising Marcia's abilities and devotion to high standards. Funeral plans in Philadelphia were pending, and there would be a memorial service in New York at a time and place to be announced.

The police were asking cooperation from all citizens, and they listed that special phone number again.

We were a somber group at the office that morning. Joe Blackwell, the managing editor, looked particularly haggard. It turned out that Lieutenant Jack Morrison had gone back to see him and had been at his apartment when his wife and children returned from their summer place. The Blackwells had rented a house for the season in Seaview on Fire Island, and usually Dotty and the kids were there all the time, with Joe going out on weekends. But Dotty had decided to come back when Joe called her about the murder, and she arrived right in the middle of Jack's questions about Joe's whereabouts on Monday night, the night of the murder. Joe had explained that he had gone to the movies by himself, but I had a sudden glimmer of what the problem was.

I happened to know that Joe was seeing Terry Kerman. Terry does photo research at Time-Life, and I had known her when we were both working in the publicity department at Doubleday, my first job in New York. I lasted only six months, and mostly I typed out itineraries for author junkets. You know, authors are always traveling around to autograph their books and appear on local television talk shows. I must have done something besides type itineraries, but that's all I remember. Everybody went to Pittsburgh to be on the Marie Torre Show and to Chicago to talk to Irv Kupcinet.

Anyway, that's how I know Terry. I didn't think anybody else knew that Joe was seeing her, though how anybody keeps anything secret from anybody else in publishing is beyond me. That's why it's better to get involved with dentists or lawyers—or possibly policemen.

It wasn't that either Joe or Terry confided in me. It's just that I had seen them the previous week, late on Thursday night at a little Hungarian restaurant on Second Avenue, and it was obvious there was something going on. My reaction to that was that Joe was a damn fool —Dotty is worth ten Terrys, and in his saner moments he must realize that. Summer bachelors are all idiots, and their girl friends are, too. I know what I'm talking about, and it's not going to happen to me again.

I had just started work on my In Box when Joe came into my office and asked me what I thought of Lieutenant Morrison.

There were several answers I could make to that, but all I said was that I thought he seemed to be very thorough and persistent.

"God, yes," Joe said. "He really put me through the wringer last night. He's got it into his head that I killed Marcia. You know I couldn't do a thing like that. Why does he go on so? Why doesn't he go after that ex-husband of hers?"

"Joe, I think they're going after everybody. You should have heard him with *me* yesterday. He even came up to my apartment just to see if my telephone was working, and I bet he's already checked out the long-distance call my parents made to me Monday night."

"Then at least you have an alibi."

"Not really. Nobody can vouch for me from about eight o'clock on. I think I'm still on his list of suspects, though probably not very high up."

"No, I'm leading the list."

"Oh, Joe, I can't really believe that."

"All those questions. At least he had the good grace not to stick around after Dotty and the kids came home. Was I relieved to see them!"

I wasn't sure whether the relief was in seeing them come or in seeing Jack Morrison leave, but I just nodded reassuringly.

"Are you going to the funeral, Karen? It's going to be in Philadelphia on Saturday, you know, and we're driving down. We can take you. We'll be back the same day."

"Yes, thanks. I was wondering how to manage transportation."

"No problem." He stood up to leave and paused by the door. "George is organizing the memorial service for next week, probably Thursday. I'm seeing him this afternoon." I said good luck, and he shrugged and left.

George T. Griffith is the president of the book-club division. He's also the man who will be appointing Marcia's successor. Joe is obviously qualified to take over, but you never know if management is going to be stupid or not. The afternoon meeting would probably just set up a temporary arrangement for running the office. We would all be stewing for weeks before they worked everything out.

I went out to lunch with three of the other editors, and we compared notes on our police interrogations. When they found out how much time Jack had spent with me (I was careful to refer to him as Lieutenant Morrison), they all began cracking jokes about me as the murderer. *They* all seemed to have solid alibis. I didn't much like being called Killer Karen, and Jerry Goulden sobered as soon as he said it. And then we all realized that this wasn't something in the endless books we read—it was real, and Marcia was dead. So we talked about Marcia and the children for a little while, and we decided that Harry would probably get custody of them, unless he had actually been the murderer. And we couldn't really believe that, any of us. Indeed, we couldn't imagine anybody we knew as a murderer, at least not as a murderer of Marcia.

"Lieutenant Morrison wanted to know if publishers get mad at us when we turn down their books," I said. "But I assured him that they don't get mad enough to kill."

That struck them all as funny, as I knew it would, and so I told them he had also wanted to know how mad we got at other book clubs when we lost a book we really wanted.

Lucy laughed and then just shook her head in wonder. "Does he really think that we're so emotionally tied up in our work that we'd kill for it? Good Lord! If I miss a needlepoint book today, there'll be another one tomorrow, sure as sunrise."

"I bet if he went to a ball game and heard somebody yelling 'Kill the umpire,' he'd want to arrest him." Jerry managed to work sports into every conversation.

"It's just that he's not familiar with publishing," I said. "We're caught up in such a tide of manuscripts and galleys that we get sort of jaded. I mean, every once in a while something comes along that I really love, but six months later I'd have a hard time remembering it."

"Trade editors are closer to their books," Rachel said. Rachel MacDowell is editor of the Biography Book Club, and she's pleasant enough, but she's older and sort of reserved and I've never gotten to know her very well. "If you're only dealing with half a dozen titles in a season," she said, "and nursing each book through copy-editing and production and sales meetings, and soothing your authors, and fighting for bigger printings and more advertising, you get more attached to individual books than we do. More involved." She had been a trade editor when she started out, and I guess she knows what she is talking about.

Jerry had been in trade, too, and he agreed. "The tough thing is dealing with authors. All those fragile egos. *They* are the ones who care passionately about their books. Maybe that's where your Lieutenant Morrison should look for his murderer."

"Marcia wrote a book once," Rachel said thoughtfully.

I didn't know that, and I said so.

22

"It must have been at least ten years ago," Rachel explained. "She had been writing short stories, you know, and had quite a few of them published. But her novel—well, it just came out and died. She didn't talk about it."

"The way *you* talk about it, Rachel, you make it sound like a dead child." Lucy looked at her curiously.

"Yes, there is a resemblance."

That seemed like a strange response, but it certainly ended speculation about Marcia's novel. Instead, we turned to speculation about Marcia's successor.

"It has to be Joe," Jerry said. "It's so obvious that he's the only one who can take over the team and make it go."

"When did you ever see George Griffith do something obvious?" I asked. "Even if he finally chooses Joe, it will be after weeks of stalling around and making us think he's going to do something else."

Rachel agreed, but she thought it would be Joe in the end, and we all hoped she was right.

It was on the tip of my tongue to ask whether Joe would want one of us as his managing editor, but I realized I would be probing a sensitive area. I thought Rachel could see herself in the job, and she probably felt she deserved it on seniority alone. (But she had been passed over when Marcia chose Joe four years ago.) And Jerry was a possible choice, too. He and Joe would make a good team. Lucy and I were too young or too new or too something to merit serious consideration, probably, and I honestly didn't want the job because it looked like too much work. Maybe some other time.

Jerry picked up the *Post* on the way back to the office, but there wasn't much new on the murder. The police had questioned some teen-agers picked up inside the service entrance of Marcia's building, but they had been let go.

"The security in that house must be terrible," Jerry said, and I agreed.

My phone was ringing and our secretary, Jerry's and mine, had disappeared again. Abby is bright and funny and capable—I just wish she were around more often. I caught the phone on the fifth ring and was surprised to find myself talking to Meredith Baker, Marcia's agent. I had met her a couple of times with Marcia and had waved at her across crowded restaurants, but I'd never had a real conversation with her.

She sounded agitated and explained why immediately: "Lieutenant Morrison was just here, and he stayed an hour. He said you gave him my name."

"Yes, Meredith. I'm sorry if he bothered you, but he asked me for the names of Marcia's friends, and of course you knew her very well, better than I did. And I knew you'd want to cooperate," I added virtuously.

"Well, of course I want him to find the wretch who killed her. But he's prying around in her past, and I don't think it's right. Can you meet me for a drink right after work? I've got to talk to somebody."

"Sure." What in the world could she have in mind? We set a time and place, and I tried to settle down to work again. It was too hard to concentrate on manuscripts, so I called in Abby and we cleared up three weeks' worth of rejection letters.

Joe Blackwell passed by my office on his way back from his meeting with George Griffith. I wondered what they had said, but I was sure that Joe had been sworn to silence. There would probably be a memo from George first thing in the morning, outlining temporary responsibilities.

When you're in a department that is part of a division that is part of a company that is part of a conglomerate, you're flooded with memos. My all-time favorite is the one that came out headed:

Re: Fly Balls

Last year the company had a picnic up in Westchester somewhere (I didn't go), and during the softball game two outfielders ran into each other and one of them was knocked out. (The other one dropped the ball and so the batter got to third base.) Two days later we all got a memo explaining how to call out for a fly ball in order to avoid future accidents. The memo was dispatched to somebody's friend at *The New Yorker,* where it was picked up and printed. Then we all got another memo explaining the confidentiality of in-house communications. There was even some talk about setting up a classification system—Secret, Top Secret, and Eyes Only. Unfortunately, common

24

sense entered in, and we went on just as sloppily as before.

Anyway, I went through my In Box and transferred most of the contents to my wastebasket. I put the rest of the stuff in my Out Box, and presumably Abby routed it properly or filed it, but I suspected a lot of it wound up in *her* wastebasket. I never pressed too hard to find out.

Then I tracked down a copy of next Sunday's *New York Times Book Review* section and skimmed through it looking for reviews of "our" books. I skipped the front page—another university-press book that would sink without a trace.

Abby was still typing my rejection letters when I left at five. I told her they could wait, but she said she was meeting somebody at six and she might as well be working because she had taken such a long lunch hour. That's what I like about publishing: it's all pretty loose, but there are enough conscientious types around to make it work.

Meredith Baker was waiting for me in the little hotel bar right across the street from her office.

She seemed to have calmed down somewhat, and maybe she was already regretting she had decided on me as her confidante. I asked for a ginger ale and she let that pass without comment, ordering a second martini for herself.

"That Lieutenant Morrison," she began. "I really think he suspected me of pulling the trigger myself. He even called Charley to confirm we were having dinner together Monday night." Charley was her husband, and they had been married for something like twenty years.

"It was my birthday and we went to Périgord," Meredith continued. "It's lucky they know me there. Imagine needing an alibi for Marcia's murder!" Her voice trembled and she was starting on her second drink. I could tell things were going to get sloppy, and I began wishing I were somewhere else, anywhere else.

"That Lieutenant Morrison," she said again. "When he couldn't pin it on me, he asked about Marcia's husband. Poor Harry." She took another gulp from her glass. "I wish they had never split up. It wasn't his idea, you know."

I murmured something soothing, but she really wasn't paying any

25

attention. She was intent on playing marriage counselor after the fact, and she rambled on and on about how they met (Marcia was a sophomore and Harry was a senior at Penn State) and what the parents thought and when they got married and how long they waited to have children.

"Marcia stayed home with the boys when they were little, you know. She had a housekeeper, but she stayed home with them anyway. And she was writing a lot then—*Cosmopolitan, McCall's*, the *Journal*. I sold everything she turned out. And then she started that damn book."

"You're the second person today who mentioned that book to me. I never heard of it before."

"*Changing Seasons*, it was called. She wrote it under her maiden name, Mary Marcia Underwood."

"I'll have to look it up," I said politely.

"It's pretty hard to find," Meredith said. "A small first printing, and they had to remainder that. Lieutenant Morrison asked me for a copy, but I didn't have one in the office and he didn't pursue it." She signaled the waiter for another drink, though she still hadn't finished her second. "That's the only thing he didn't pursue, though. Do you know that man is after every detail of Marcia's sex life? Do you think he's a pervert?"

"Oh, Meredith!"

"Don't 'Oh, Meredith' me. You weren't there. He asked me about Marty Bayliss."

"I told him that Marty used to take her to publishing parties and they were good friends. And he figured out, just from the tone of my voice, I guess, that Marty's queer."

"Yes. So then he wanted to know if Marcia was a lesbian!"

"What an idiot. But then"—why was I trying to defend him?—"he didn't know her."

"That's right. I told him he was crazy, but then I made the mistake of telling him about Ted Ferris."

Meredith was on her third martini by then, or I don't suppose she would have told me. And told me at such length. Ted was Marcia's lawyer when she filed for divorce, and I gathered from Meredith that he had become Marcia's lover, too. It went on for quite a while, and they had only broken off three weeks ago.

"He found somebody else," Meredith said. "Another divorce client, as a matter of fact. Marcia wasn't the first, and this new one won't be the last. He's in a perfect spot, you know. A woman is terribly vulnerable when her marriage is breaking up, and her lawyer can be such a calm, steadying influence."

I finished off my ginger ale and considered the situation. "Meredith, do you think he killed her?"

"What do you mean?"

"Do you think Ted Ferris killed Marcia?" He was the best suspect so far, I thought.

"Why would he do that? He walked out on her three weeks ago. It's true that Marcia was very upset that day. But then she calmed down; you know the way she is. The way she was. No, maybe three weeks ago she was mad enough to kill him, but not now. And there'd be no reason for *him* to kill *her.*"

"No, I guess not." I had a feeling we were missing something, but I didn't know quite what. I looked at my watch, rather pointedly, and Meredith decided she had had enough. I poured her into a cab (she lives in the Village) and walked over to take the bus home.

I was just finishing the dishes and had started to defrost the refrigerator when the doorbell rang. I buzzed back to see who it was, but I had already guessed: Lieutenant Jack Morrison. I was wearing my rattiest blue jeans and an old T-shirt; defrosting the refrigerator always winds up being a sloppy job and invariably I spill something and wind up scrubbing the kitchen floor. Anyway, there was no time to change my clothes, and he was rapping on my door by the time I had run a comb through my hair. Serves him right—people ought to phone ahead.

He came in, apologizing for disturbing me, saying he had just a few questions. He looked around and then sat down at my desk and pulled out that damned notebook again. I perched on the arm of a chair, ready to dash to the kitchen when the ice started melting, and Jack just gave me a puzzled look.

"I phoned you last night," he began conversationally, "but there wasn't any answer."

"I was out."

"Yes, I guessed that. Where were you?"

"You mean I have to tell you about last night, too? Was there another murder?"

"No, no. I didn't mean to sound as if I'm interrogating you. This is unofficial."

I stared rather pointedly at his notebook, and he had the good grace to look embarrassed.

"Oh, never mind." I got up and turned down the radio and fiddled with the window air-conditioner, which had developed a strange new rattle. "I went upstairs to talk to Elly Crawford, and then we walked over to Eighty-sixth Street to see the new Robert Redford movie. I had a hamburger afterward. Call Elly—she'll bear me out. I may even have a ticket stub around somewhere."

"Please, Karen, I don't suspect you of anything. I believe you when you say you went to the movies last night. I'm sure you didn't kill Marcia. Now will you just sit down and relax for a minute? That's better. Was it a good movie? Frankly, I've never quite understood the fuss about Robert Redford."

"That's what Joe Blackwell said, too. He saw it at a screening last week and he fell asleep."

"A screening?" There was something peculiar about the way Jack said that, but I didn't catch it immediately.

"Yes, Marcia couldn't go and she passed her invitation on to him." Jack still looked blank.

"The studios hold private screenings of new pictures, and some editors are on the invitation lists," I explained. "You get to go free, and it's sort of fun. There are always other people from publishing there."

"I see." He looked like the cat that swallowed the cream. "So if Joe Blackwell went to a screening last week and didn't much like the picture, isn't it strange that he would pay money to go see the very same thing again on Monday night?"

Dear God, I had just wrecked Joe's alibi. What a dumb lie to get himself caught in. I couldn't think of any way to retrieve the situation at all.

"Karen, I said don't you think it's strange that Joe went to see

28

the same movie again Monday night."

"He could have changed his mind." It sounded lame to me, too.

"You know better than that. He's seeing some girl, isn't that it? While his wife is out on Fire Island, he's been playing around. You know who she is, Karen—it's written all over your face."

"I think you had better talk to Joe about that."

"I will. But, Karen, we're involved in a murder case. Remember that."

"I can't believe that Joe killed Marcia."

"Maybe he didn't. But he's going to be better off telling me the truth about what's going on. When you talk to him about this, and I can see that you're going to, would you please tell him to open up and tell me who the girl is?"

I nodded. What a wretched, stupid business.

"Karen, it's not you, is it?"

I was absolutely speechless. If there had been anything to throw, I'd have hit him with it.

"I'm sorry, Karen. I can see that it isn't. God, are you ever going to forgive me when all this is over?"

At that moment there was a loud crash from the kitchen, and he jumped a foot. I think he even reached for his gun, but I couldn't be sure. To tell the truth, it shook me up a little, too.

"I'm defrosting the refrigerator," I explained a little shakily. "I think a big piece of ice crashed down." That's what it was. I wiped up the mess and dislodged the rest of the ice while he hung around in the kitchen doorway looking embarrassed again.

The phone rang and I asked him to get it.

"Won't it seem strange if a man answers?"

"Would you rather come in here and wipe up the floor?"

He retreated hastily and picked up the receiver in the bedroom, and I knew immediately I had made a mistake: it was my parents in Neenah, Wisconsin, and it took Jack five minutes to explain who he was and what he was doing there.

"No, she's all right, Mrs. Lindstrom, Mr. Lindstrom. . . . I'm a policeman. A New York City policeman. Lieutenant Jack Morrison . . . Morrison. M O R R I S O N . . . Not exactly. My grandfather was Jewish. The rest is sort of a mixture, English and Scotch-Irish. . . .

29

Yes, I'm glad to meet you, too. . . . Danish, that's interesting. And Swedish on your mother's side. . . . Yes, I met her yesterday. She's safe, Mrs. Lindstrom. Really. She's right here."

He was sweating by then, and I finally took pity on him and accepted the receiver from his willing hand.

"Hi, Mother, Dad. I'm fine. Not murdered at all. . . . He's just asking me questions, Mother. He's in the middle of an investigation. . . . No, I don't think he has solved the case yet." I looked over at Jack. "Have you found a clue, Lieutenant? My mother wants to know."

"A clue? What does she mean, a clue?" He shook his head. "Tell her—tell her we have some promising leads."

I relayed that. "No, Dad, I'm perfectly all right. . . . No, I don't think I should ask for round-the-clock protection. . . . No, I would *not* want a policeman with me twenty-four hours a day."

Jack started to laugh, and he retreated toward the kitchen so they wouldn't hear him.

"Of course he knows what he's doing. He's a veteran, been on the force more than ten years. . . . I can't help it if he sounded flustered when you called. I was defrosting the refrigerator, and this chunk of ice . . . Oh, never mind. I'm all right. Really, I am. I feel perfectly safe. . . . Sure, I'll call as soon as he captures the murderer. You can depend on me. Thanks for calling. I'm fine. I'm really fine. Good-by."

I hung up, giddy with repressed laughter, fizzing up now like bubbles of champagne. Jack smiled at me across the length of the living room, and for a minute the case melted away and he almost forgot he was a cop. But then he reined himself in—I could see it happening—and we went back to that old question-and-answer routine.

"I forgot to ask you something," he said, opening his notebook again. We sat down facing each other across my desk, and he picked up his pen. "Did Marcia fire anybody recently? Are there any former members of the staff who could bear a grudge?"

I wrenched my thoughts back to the office staff and tried to be helpful. "She's never fired any editors that I can think of. Penny left two years ago because she was going back to graduate school—that's when I took over MSI. And Sam decided he really liked magazines better and got himself transferred to *American World.*"

30

Jack looked blank, so I explained. "Readers' Circle Book Club Division is part of the Berwyn Publishing Company. Berwyn has a string of magazines, most of them pretty specialized, but *American World* is on the newsstands, a big, glossy picture magazine. Normally there isn't much transferring back and forth between the divisions of Berwyn, but it has been done. Sam went to the magazines, and one of our club editors came from Berwyn Paperbacks. Berwyn is huge —book clubs, paperbacks, magazines, trade books, and educational materials. And over Berwyn is Phoenix Industries, a conglomerate with paper mills and printing plants and office machines, and maybe even shoes and ships and sealing wax, for all I know."

"Maybe I should look at an organization chart," Jack said, but he didn't sound as if he meant it. "The point is that Marcia didn't fire anybody recently."

"No. . . . No, that's not quite right. Come to think of it, she fired Rachel's secretary six months ago. A crazy kid. Shirley something. She lived in the East Village and she was all wrapped up with some guy from South America—from Colombia, I think it was. She went around the office with a blank expression on her face, and maybe she was strung out on drugs. I don't know. That's what Abby said once. My secretary, Abby Wiggins. She knew her a little better than the rest of us."

"Strung out on drugs," Jack said thoughtfully. "With a boy friend from Colombia. You don't know his name?"

"No. Abby probably does. I'd phone her right now, but I happen to know she's out for the evening."

"I'll call her in the morning," Jack said. "I don't understand why Marcia fired this secretary. Why didn't the girl's own boss do it? Rachel, you said her name was?"

"Yes. Rachel MacDowell. You must have talked to her in the office yesterday. An older woman. She handles the Biography Book Club."

"Oh, sure." Jack riffled back through his notebook. "She was home with her husband Monday night. I remember her. Why didn't she handle the firing herself?"

"I don't know. She was on vacation, I think. And I suppose Rachel wasn't very keen on the idea of firing Shirley anyway. Shirley Hastings, her name was. I just remembered. I think Rachel had some vague idea she could straighten the girl out. But Shirley was really asking to be fired. She didn't even come in half the time."

"Still, it's rather strange. To come back from vacation and find your secretary has been fired. How did Rachel react?"

"I don't know. She didn't make any production of it. Just a little more tight-lipped than usual. They were reshuffling some of the secretaries, reducing staff, and Rachel is sharing with Lucy now. It seems to be working out."

Jack continued to look puzzled. "There's something peculiar about this whole incident. Still, it was six months ago, so maybe it doesn't mean much. Rachel MacDowell—does she get along with the rest of the staff? Did she like Marcia?"

"I think so. She came along to lunch with Jerry and Lucy and me today. She's been around in publishing for a long time and knows everybody. She even knew that Marcia had written a book, which is more than I did."

"Oh, yes. That book. I must get hold of it. Maybe there's a copy in Marcia's apartment."

"Why in the world would you want a copy? She wrote it ten years ago, and I gather it was a big flop. They remaindered the first printing, according to her agent."

"Her agent," Jack echoed. "The emotional Mrs. Meredith Baker. So she phoned you after I was there."

"Yes. How did you guess?"

"I had mentioned your name, and I had the feeling that she would want to compare notes on her interview with somebody. Was she very upset?"

"We met after work and she had three martinis. She thinks you are a sex pervert."

Jack laughed. "I could see that mention of lesbianism shocked her. But sometimes if you accuse somebody of something outrageous, you'll get the real story on something else. You know, you'll bring a guy in for bank robbery and he'll confess to purse-snatching instead. Mrs. Baker had to prove that Marcia was straight, so she told me about . . . Well, never mind."

"She told me, too."

"After three martinis, she would. So, what do you think?"

32

"That lecherous lawyer. He's the one you ought to go after. He sounds more like a murderer than anyone else."

"Three weeks after he broke off with her? And why should *he* want to kill *her?*"

"I don't know. Blackmail? Maybe Marcia knew something he didn't want her to tell anybody."

"So he came to her apartment, and she let him in, and he walked into her bedroom to get her gun (because he hadn't thought to bring a weapon with him), and then he shot her."

"I don't know. Maybe. Or maybe she phoned him to see him one last time, and when she couldn't get him back, she decided to shoot him. But he got the gun away from her and killed her. It sounds a lot more logical to me than accusing poor Joe Blackwell."

"You have a vivid imagination, Karen. Or you've read too many mysteries. But don't worry about it. We're investigating the elusive Mr. Ferris, too."

"Elusive?"

"He seems to be on vacation. He drove off to . . . Never mind. We're looking into the matter."

It didn't seem fair that he was insisting on knowing everything I knew, but he wouldn't tell me anything I couldn't read in the papers.

He went back to Meredith Baker again, but I couldn't think of anything else she had told me. He asked me if anything else had come up at lunch, and I racked my brains.

"We were speculating about what would happen to Marcia's children, Tim and Hank."

"Do you know them?"

"Yes, I spent a weekend with them, Marcia and both boys, on Nantucket. We bicycled all over the place. It was Memorial Day, seven weeks ago, and we flew up for four days. They're nice kids. I suppose Harry will get custody. Unless you think *he* killed her."

Jack refused to comment.

"I don't know what else happened at lunch. We all decided Joe Blackwell should be promoted. Unless you want to make *him* the murderer again. No? What else . . . ? Rachel told us about Marcia's book. But I told you that. She talked about it in such a strange way, though, as if the book had been a child that died or something. I don't

33

know. We're all on edge, I guess, going from talk about death to silly graveyard humor to office politics again. I'd like to be leading a nice, normal life again. How do you stand it all the time?"

"You put up some kind of buffer, I think. Or I try to. I don't want to get completely callous, but I suppose I have, to some extent. Anyway, most murders aren't like this one, you know. There's usually no mystery about them. Somebody gets drunk in a bar and pulls a knife, or an outraged husband goes after his wife's boy friend, or something like that. It's usually pretty open-and-shut, a matter of finding witnesses who will talk. Cases like this one are exceptional. We have to go very carefully, and everybody gets edgy with the press breathing down our necks. But don't worry, Karen, we'll solve it. I wasn't really joking when I told you to tell your mother we have some leads." He put away his notebook and stood up, dominating the living room again.

I walked him to the door and we shook hands, very formally. He said he'd telephone if he had any more questions, and he promised not to walk in on any more refrigerators defrosting. His smile was endearing and almost civilian, but the rest of him was strictly cop. And so he left.

Absolutely maddening. I went out to the kitchen and filled all the ice-cube trays, and then I went to bed.

I got to work early next morning because I wanted to talk to Joe Blackwell before everybody else wandered in. He was surprised to see me in his office, and he started to make some joke about how he was going to crack the whip and install time clocks, but I cut him off by closing the door. Closed doors are significant in our world, usually associated with promotions, firings, or resignations, though occasionally other secrets are exchanged. If we were going to be talking about murder alibis and extramarital affairs, we needed privacy.

"Lieutenant Morrison came to see me last night," I began

Joe went rigid and broke the pencil he had been fussing with. Ever since he gave up smoking, he's had this terrible problem of what to do with his hands. His secretary came back from vacation in Greece last month and gave him some worry beads, but he said they reminded him of Captain Queeg, and he took them home to his six-year-old.

"Joe, I don't know how to tell you this, but I'm afraid I wrecked your story about Monday night. You see, I was telling Lieutenant Morrison about seeing that Robert Redford movie, and I told him you had fallen asleep in it when you went to the screening. So he asked why you had gone to see it again Monday and paid money for it if you hadn't liked it the first time, and I couldn't think of anything to answer at all."

"Oh, God."

"Joe, I'm sorry. He trapped me, and I didn't know what you had told him."

"Sure, Karen, I'm not blaming you. It's just . . . God, how did I get myself into this?" He swiveled his chair around to look out the window, away from me.

"Lieutenant Morrison," I began again, tentatively.

"What about him?"

No way to say it roundabout, just blurt it out. "He thinks you're seeing some girl, and your wife doesn't know, and that's why you told him that story about the movie."

There was a long pause, and then Joe turned back to face me. "Clever, clever Lieutenant Morrison. The only thing he's wrong about is that Dotty knows. She guessed. And you know, too, and maybe everybody does. George Griffith, too."

"No, I don't think so. Certainly *I* haven't told anybody. But I guessed, Joe. I saw you with Terry in that Hungarian restaurant on Second Avenue last week, and it just looked to me as if . . ."

"You even know who it is. Oh, hell, what a goddamn mess. What is Morrison going to do?"

"He wants you to call him, give him a straight story. This is a murder case, after all. Joe, I'm sure he doesn't think you killed Marcia, but if you don't tell him the truth, he's going to go prying into the whole situation, and then it will all come out."

He contemplated that bleak possibility and shuddered. "The really dumb thing is that I've screwed up everything with Dotty, too. She's talking divorce. I don't want a divorce. I don't want to marry Terry Kerman. I don't even . . . Oh, hell. Do you really think I have to call Lieutenant Morrison?"

I nodded and wrote down the phone number the police had listed in the papers. Joe stared at it bleakly. He was still staring at it when I excused myself and left.

Joe's secretary looked at me curiously (that closed-door syndrome), but I just wished her good morning and headed back for my office.

Abby had left me a stack of neatly typed rejection letters—she had finished them all the night before—but I had long since signed them when she breezed in, twenty minutes later than usual.

"Hi, Karen. You'll never guess who woke me up this morning."

I had a hunch who did, but I waited for her to tell me.

"Lieutenant Morrison. Jack. We're on a first-name basis now, isn't that funny?"

36

"Hilarious. What happened?"

"Wait till I tell you." She was going to make a production of it, sitting down across from me and getting comfortable in my visitor's chair. "Well, he phoned me a little after eight and woke me up. Karen, I think there's something the matter with my clock radio. It didn't go on, and that's the third time that's happened. Jack looked at it when he came up, but he didn't know how to fix it, either."

I blinked at that, but she went on blithely.

"Anyway, on the phone he asked if he could see me before I went to work. He didn't want to come to the office and disrupt anything. Wasn't that thoughtful of him?"

"The soul of courtesy, Lieutenant Morrison."

"So I invited him over for breakfast. He'd already eaten, he said, but when he came up, he had a cup of coffee with me. Two cups. He says I make good coffee. He's tired of instant, and I had made a whole pot." She was very pleased with herself.

"Where were your roommates?"

Abby lives down in the Village with two other girls; I think they had all been in college together.

"Chrissy is away on vacation, and Mary works down on Wall Street and had to leave before Jack arrived. She was sorry to miss him."

"A real pity."

Abby looked at me as if I had said something strange, and then she went on. "Jack wanted to know all about Shirley Hastings. You remember her? She was Rachel's secretary, and Marcia fired her."

"I remember."

"That's what he wanted to know about. And Ricardo, too. Ricardo Raúl Gómez, her boy friend. I hadn't talked to either of them for months. But I told Jack everything I could remember. Shirley was always kind of strange, I thought. Ray and I went out to dinner with them once. That's before I broke up with Ray, of course."

"Of course."

"Shirley went to work for an advertising agency after she left us. Did you know that? I talked to her a couple of times and she liked it, I think. Raymond and Lee, it's called. I think I'll phone and see if she's still there."

I nodded agreement.

"I'm not sure if Shirley is still involved with Ricardo," Abby continued. "I never could figure him out at all. He always had money, but he didn't seem to work."

"Maybe he comes from a wealthy family," I said.

"Jack suggested that, too. Isn't that strange, how your minds work alike?"

"Passing strange. What else?"

"You know, I think you're right. About the wealthy family. Ricardo knew a lot of diplomats and couriers and people like that. He even took Shirley to some big bash at the United Nations once. Shirley tried out her college French, but nobody understood her."

"Lieutenant Morrison would understand her. He would read her like a book."

"Karen, you're saying the most peculiar things this morning. Right off the wall."

"Sorry. I'm just fascinated by your conversation with Lieutenant Morrison, that's all. What else came out about the case?"

"He asked about Ricardo's friends, but I hadn't met any of them. That's about it. He said I shouldn't broadcast it around, what we talked about, but I could tell you because he was sure you'd want to know and you would get it out of me."

"How right he is. Thank you."

"Karen, I don't understand how all this about Shirley and Ricardo fits in with Marcia's murder, do you?"

"Not really, no. But Lieutenant Morrison is very thorough, and he follows through on everything."

"I guess you're right. Did you know he majored in psychology at Queens College?"

"I think he's probably got his master's and doctorate by now."

"Oh. Well, he didn't mention that."

"Modest, too. Abby, why don't you call Shirley at that advertising agency and see if she's still there?"

"All right. Do you want to talk to her?"

"No. I'm just sort of curious to see if she's there. That's all."

"OK. What shall I say to her?"

"I don't know. Suggest you have lunch together or something."

But Shirley wasn't there. Abby came in and quoted the personnel director of the advertising agency: "Miss Hastings is no longer in our employ. She was terminated two weeks ago, and we do not know if she has another job."

"That sounds pretty chilly."

"I could try calling her at home," Abby volunteered.

But it turned out that Shirley's home phone had been disconnected, and there was a recorded announcement to say so.

Lieutenant Jack Morrison was probably checking out her family by now or looking in the morgue or something. He had a whole police department to help him.

But it turned out that I had assistance, too. Abby's curiosity had been fired, and she was hot on the scent. That's why she told me about her friend Reba Belknap in personnel. Reba had access to all Berwyn Publishing Company records, and there would surely be a card on Shirley Hastings, including such pertinent information as the person to be notified in case of emergency.

Abby was gone half an hour, and Jerry Goulden came in and complained to me for the fortieth time that she was never at her desk. I said she was working on a project for me, so he went off to the Xerox room himself, grumbling mildly. I'm sure it could have waited, whatever it was.

Abby came back, beaming, holding a Xerox copy of Shirley's file card. "I ran into Jerry in the Xerox room, but I wouldn't tell him what I had been doing. I swore Reba to secrecy, too."

"Fine. We'll dream up a password, too." From the card I learned that Shirley's next of kin was her father, Harold Hastings, who lived in Massapequa, Long Island. Abby phoned, but there was no answer. She was going to identify herself as a friend who was trying to get in touch with Shirley to have lunch. That was true enough. She tried periodically for the rest of the day, but there was no answer. Well, maybe Mr. Hastings was away—at work, or on vacation, or in the hospital, or anything.

When I came back from lunch, the copies of George Griffith's memo had been distributed to everybody in the book-club division. It was President George T. Griffith at his most pompous and stuffy. Most of the memo dealt with the memorial service for Marcia, scheduled for next Thursday, together with a new statement about Marcia's high standards and our grief over her loss and the problem of trying to replace her.

In this difficult transitional period, Joseph Blackwell will be assuming additional duties temporarily, working closely with me on all major decisions that affect the future of the editorial department.

Mr. Blackwell has been authorized to take over the day-to-day functioning of the department, including all routine financial disbursements.

I am sure we will all cooperate to assure the continuing excellence of the editorial decision-making process.

Big deal: Joe could now sign our expense-account slips, and he had to go running to George for everything else. George hadn't even given him the title of acting editor-in-chief. Could he possibly have heard that Joe was running around with Terry? No, and it wouldn't bother him in any case. Maybe, though, George had decided not to make any commitments until Marcia's murder had been cleared up. Until the police arrested someone, George wouldn't want to take the chance that his choice for editor-in-chief was a murder suspect. Still, it was a terrible spot for Joe. In effect, he was still managing editor, with most of the duties of editorial director added on, but without the authority or the title or any added perks. And his marriage was shaky and he was in trouble with the police. No wonder he started smoking again; he needed all the consolation he could get.

I surprised him lighting up a cigarette when I passed his office later that afternoon, and I commented on this fall from grace.

He looked ruefully at his ashtray. Four stubs in it already. "My first pack in seven months. When I think how I struggled . . . Maybe when all this is over I'll have the strength of my doctor's convictions again, but I need something to get me through this week, and maybe next, and the one after that."

I nodded sympathetically. I kicked the habit two years ago—two years, two months, and one day—and it was absurdly painful at first.

Joe eyed the door for a moment. He refrained from closing it—too many closed doors make people nervous. But he chose his words

40

carefully when he spoke again, and his voice was so low I had to strain to hear.

"Karen, I followed your advice. The lieutenant was quite . . . reasonable. He said he would be very discreet in checking out my whereabouts, and if he can confirm what I told him, there won't be anything to worry about. I think he disapproves of me, though." Joe crushed out his cigarette and then almost immediately pulled out another one. "He's a strange guy for a cop."

I agreed, but I had had enough of Lieutenant Jack Morrison at second hand, and I changed the subject. "I read George's memo," I began.

Joe's face closed up immediately, and he pushed back his chair and stood up. "We all have a lot of hard work ahead of us, Karen."

It was meant as an exit line for me, so I agreed hastily and left. Joe was obviously furious and didn't want to talk about it. And I should have known better. We were in for a rough few weeks.

I settled down with a manuscript and had finally managed to lose myself in the plot by the end of the day. I was actually startled when Abby stuck her head in the door to say good night.

"There's still no answer at the Hastingses' " she said. "I'll try again in the morning."

"Fine. Thanks a lot. See you tomorrow."

It occurred to me that Mr. Hastings—and Mrs. Hastings, too, if there was such a person—might be at home tonight and gone again tomorrow, so I made a note of the phone number and tucked it in my wallet.

On impulse I checked out the Manhattan phone directory for a Ricardo Raúl Gómez, and there was one on Madison Avenue. It seemed an unlikely address for him somehow, but Madison Avenue isn't really out of my way going home, even through it does mean two bus fares instead of one.

I hadn't actually planned to do more than ride by, but there were two police cars in front of Ricardo's building. I couldn't resist, so I pulled the cord on the bus and got off. If I stayed across the street and walked back slowly, maybe I would see the police arrest somebody.

Nothing happened. I spotted a coffee shop with a clear view of the building entrance, so I went in and positioned myself by the window, ordering coffee from the languid waitress. I didn't really care about rapid service, and it might be a long wait.

Actually, it was twenty minutes before anything happened, and then it wasn't much. Some cops hurried out of the building and hustled a very angry man into the back seat of one of the police cars. They gunned the motor and drove away. A few minutes later a couple of plainclothes men emerged, and I recognized one of them. For one awful moment I thought they were looking around for a place to have a cup of coffee, and then they seemed to be arguing about something, and finally Jack shrugged and they both got in the other car and took off.

I paid my bill and got out of there. I had lost all desire to call the Hastingses that night. Let Abby play detective in the morning.

There was nothing in the *Times* the next morning, Friday morning, that seemed to have any relationship at all to that arrest, or whatever it was, on Madison Avenue. But I was startled to see a small story on an inside page about the police finding the body of an unidentified young woman in the trunk of a stolen car in a Brooklyn parking lot. Captain Frank Reilly was declining to comment again, and there was another telephone number for anyone with information about the case.

How many Captain Frank Reillys could there be in the New York City police department, and if he was the same one involved in the investigation of Marcia's murder, what was he doing in Brooklyn? Unless the two cases were connected . . . Which made me wonder if that could be the body of Shirley Hastings found in the trunk of the car.

I kept that grim thought to myself. More than ever I wanted Abby to make that phone call to the Hastings residence in Massapequa, but I didn't want her getting emotional and upsetting whoever answered the telephone.

I found it difficult to concentrate during editorial meeting that morning. Joe presided in Marcia's place, grim reminder of her absence. But it wasn't precedent-making: Joe had run the meeting on other occasions in the past, when Marcia was on vacation or attending an agency presentation or something. He wound it up in record time, less than an hour, partly because we had all read fewer books than usual that week; besides, nobody had much heart for the usual jokes and wisecracks.

Abby was waiting for me when I got back to my office, and she was full of news. "I called Massapequa and the phone rang and rang, and finally this breathless woman answered the phone. Mrs. Dimaria. She's Shirley's aunt, and she had just stopped by the house to water the plants and make sure that everything was all right. Wasn't I lucky to reach her! She says the whole family is on vacation, driving through Canada. She had a postcard from the Gaspé Peninsula. And she doesn't think Shirley is with them, but she doesn't know for sure. The only phone number she has for Shirley is the one I have, the one that's been disconnected. Mrs. Dimaria was surprised to hear that. I don't think she's seen her lately."

Abby was very pleased with her detective work, and I complimented her.

"I have another idea," she said. "I looked up Ricardo in the phone book, and I thought I'd call him and ask if he knows where Shirley is. What do you think?"

I didn't quite know how to answer that, but she was eager and I couldn't see what harm it would do. I wasn't surprised, though, when there was no answer to her call.

Abby popped in again with the rest of her messages. "Your lunch date is confirmed at Madrigal for twelve thirty. And you have to call Morrow about that mystery you made an offer on. And Lieutenant Jack Morrison called to say that he would probably be seeing you at the funeral in Philadelphia tomorrow. Isn't that a surprise? Why do you suppose he's going?"

"I don't know. Maybe he thinks the murderer will step forward and confess."

"No. He knows better than that," Abby said thoughtfully. "But somebody might do something suspicious. You be sure to watch everybody and let me know."

I promised, and she left me to make my phone calls.

++++++++

4

++++++++

Marcia's funeral was scheduled for Saturday, near Philadelphia, and only a small contingent was going from New York. That's really why the memorial service had been scheduled—for the benefit of her New York friends. I might not have made the trip myself, but when Joe offered transportation, it seemed like a good idea to go.

The drive down to Philadelphia that morning is not something that lingers pleasantly in my memory. It was a gray and drizzly day, and the barren wastes of the New Jersey oil-refinery country depressed us all. I was in the back seat with Meredith Baker, who had invited herself along at the last minute. She had planned to make the trip with her husband, she explained, but Charley was coming down with a summer cold and didn't feel up to the drive. Besides, he hadn't really known Marcia that well, Meredith rambled on. Not the way she, Meredith, had known her, dating all the way back to summer camp in the Adirondacks when Marcia was ten and Meredith was twelve. Meredith remembered meeting her in Cabin 7 and showing her where to stow her gear. She even remembered teaching her the camp song, all of them from Cabin 7, sitting around the campfire one night. And then, unlikely as it sounds, Meredith proceeded to sing it for all of us. And she hadn't even been drinking.

Joe Blackwell, who was driving, was glum and silent, and Dotty Blackwell, sitting beside him in the front seat, was elaborately polite whenever she had to speak to him. That was for Meredith's benefit, I guess, and mine, too, because of course Joe hadn't told Dotty that I knew their marriage was in a fragile state. So Dotty was play-acting for Meredith, but I had to pretend to believe her, too, and Joe knew that I knew, and it was all too complicated and uncomfortable. Only Meredith, chattering on and on about her early days in New York, seemed oblivious to the tension. I made the right responses and occasionally asked a question, but Meredith seemed to be perfectly at ease with her monologue, and I had half tuned her out until she mentioned the murder and said Lieutenant Morrison had called her again.

That jolted the front-seat occupants into attention, too, and Joe stirred out of his silence. "But Meredith, *why* does he want a copy of Marcia's book? She wrote it ten years ago, and I never even heard of it until this week. It's not as if it were on her mind or as if she had talked about it constantly."

"Jerry Goulden compared it to a ballplayer's fumble," I said. "A player talks about the scores he makes, not his errors."

"Oh, it wasn't that bad," Meredith said. "Though, frankly, I read it so long ago that I don't remember it very well. Something about a family in a small town, and the father is away at war, and they all change and grow up and move away."

"It sounds like a lot of other books," I said. "We turn down that story at least once a month in the clubs."

"Exactly," Joe said. "So why do the police want to see it?"

"I don't know," Meredith said, "but I scouted around my apartment and couldn't find it. Maybe it's in that pile of books we took out to Amagansett at the beginning of the summer." Meredith and Charley had a vacation house in eastern Long Island, but they had sublet it for the month of July. "I told Lieutenant Morrison I'd look for it next month, and he seemed disappointed."

"Marcia must have had a copy," Joe said. "Why doesn't Morrison just go through her bookcases and borrow it?"

"He looked," Meredith replied, "but he couldn't find it."

"It's all much ado about nothing, if you ask me," Dotty said, coming into the conversation for the first time since she had given map directions an hour earlier. "I think the cops are handling the case very badly. Prying into all sorts of things that don't concern them, looking for old books. Idiotic. Why don't they just find out who hated the poor woman enough to kill her? I can't imagine that she had made that many enemies in her life."

"Marcia didn't have an enemy in the world," Meredith objected.

"Then why was she killed?" Dotty said.

That shut us all up for a few miles.

"About the book," Joe began again, tentatively. "Was it at all autobiographical? Could it have betrayed some family secret?"

Meredith considered that at length before she commented. "Most first novels are autobiographical to some degree, but I can't think of any dire family secrets betrayed."

"And it's ten years after the fact," Dotty objected. "If anybody felt betrayed, why should he wait ten years to take revenge?"

"Maybe he just read it recently," Joe said.

"But the book has been dead ten years. Who's going to worry about it now?" Dotty shook her head and then looked disapprovingly at Joe, who was lighting up his sixth cigarette. "I think your Lieutenant Morrison is a poor excuse for a detective."

"He's not *my* Lieutenant Morrison," Joe objected.

"Or mine," Meredith agreed fervently. "Going around prying into things he shouldn't. Libeling the dead."

They seemed to expect me to agree with them, but I gave them something else to chew on. "He's going to be at the funeral today. Lieutenant Morrison. Here in Philadelphia."

"I think that's very bad taste," Meredith said. "Really, Karen, wouldn't you think the man would show a little more consideration than that?"

"It's part of his job, I guess. He's still trying to find out who murdered her, after all."

"Well, the murderer won't be coming to the funeral," Meredith said. "Stupid waste of time. Waste of taxpayers' money, too. No wonder the city can't pay its bills. The waste in government is positively appalling."

Meredith had found a new subject for a monologue, and the rest of us lapsed into silence for the next hour.

We had some difficulty finding the church, which was not in Philadelphia but in a suburb on the Main Line, one of those unpronounceable Welsh names. The service was just starting as we arrived, and I looked around for familiar faces. The only people I recognized were Marcia's boys, Tim and Hank, and their father, Harry Richardson.

They were in the front pew, beside an erect gray-haired woman who was, I presumed, Marcia's mother. Then the couple with her must be Marcia's brother and sister-in-law from Connecticut. The others were more distant relatives, I supposed, and local friends. Not many. Marcia hadn't lived here for more than twenty years, not since she first went away to college.

I had a few morbid thoughts about how many people would remember me in Wisconsin in another ten years, and I was feeling pretty weepy by the time the organist struck up the recessional. It wasn't until then that I spotted Jack Morrison, who had been half concealed in the alcove where they had the baptismal font. He was talking earnestly to another man who looked vaguely familiar, Captain Frank Reilly. Jack caught my eye and nodded and came over afterward, while we were all assembled on the church steps waiting to get the cars lined up for the trip to the cemetery. He introduced Frank Reilly, leaving out the title, but in spite of the fact that Frank was in plain-clothes, he had cop written all over him. Jack seemed to blend in with the crowd a little better.

I introduced myself to Marcia's mother, Mrs. Underwood; and the boys, Tim and Hank, made a fuss over me. I think they were glad to see a familiar face, and one that reminded them of happier times somewhere else. We *had* had a good time bicycling in Nantucket. Then they went off with their grandmother to the first car, and after a little shuffling around, the procession got under way and we drove to the cemetery.

We were all standing around sort of awkwardly at the grave site, after the interment service, when Mrs. Underwood, obviously at the prompting of Tim and Hank, suggested that I come back with them to the house for some coffee. I was starting to explain that I had driven down with friends and there would be a problem about transportation home when Jack materialized at my elbow and said that was no problem at all: he had his car and could take me.

Mrs. Underwood turned to him with a grateful smile. "Lieutenant Morrison, how nice of you. I want *you* to come to the house, too. I have that copy of Marcia's book for you. And the boys will be so happy to spend a little time with you, Karen."

So the master psychologist had been at it again. Jack was all charm and politesse, but there was a gleam of laughter in his dark eyes as he watched me explain to Joe and Dotty and Meredith that I wouldn't be driving back with them. Well, that would give Meredith plenty of grist for a whole new monologue. Would she cast me as the murderer, I wondered, spotted by a clever policeman, or would she decide I had fallen into the lecherous clutches of a sex pervert?

Frank Reilly had already disappeared—he was checking into some local records, Jack explained—when Tim and Hank rushed over, volunteering to come along with us in Jack's car and direct us to the Underwood house. But I think they were disappointed; they had half expected the car to be equipped with a police radio and maybe even disappearing machine guns, *à la* James Bond, but it was just an ordinary year-old Chevrolet.

Jack let them examine his police identification, though, and he promised to show them a real police car back in New York, so of course they were won over. And he easily extracted from them all conceivably relevant information. They had been notified of their mother's death Tuesday afternoon. Their father had called them. And then Aunt Pat and Uncle Bill had driven over from Hartford and picked them up and taken them to New York the next day. They were staying with their father, but they thought they would probably be going back to camp to finish out the month of July. And they were staying overnight here with their Grandma Underwood. Yes, their father was there, too.

It struck me that Harry was on remarkably good terms with his ex-mother-in-law, but that was certainly to the credit of both of them. Actually, Marcia and Harry had had a fairly civilized divorce, when you come right down to it. He was a most unlikely suspect. I wondered if Jack was thinking the same thing.

We weren't the only guests at the Underwoods'. A dozen relatives and neighbors had followed along from the cemetery, and the atmosphere was friendly, almost cheerful.

Mrs. Underwood greeted us and sent Tim upstairs to retrieve her copy of Marcia's book. She was still a little puzzled by Jack's request to borrow it. "It wasn't very successful, you know, and she was terribly disappointed. Nine months of her life to produce it, and she always said it was the most uncomfortable pregnancy she ever had. Her short stories came to her so easily, you see, and they all sold for quite a lot of money."

"I'm very much interested in reading it anyway, Mrs. Underwood," Jack said, "and of course I'll return it to you as soon as I can."

She nodded, still bemused. "I can't begin to imagine how it fits in with this vicious murder. I looked through it again after you telephoned. The family seems somewhat idealized, except for the father, but I always thought it was a fine portrait of a time and place, something to be cherished."

"It was the only novel she wrote, I understand," Jack said.

"That's right. She decided to get back into editing after that. She said it was less . . . involving. I always thought she worked too hard, though. Too many hours a day. Not that she neglected her family, of course," Mrs. Underwood added loyally. "But I don't think Harry understood her success. She was the first woman to be editorial director of Readers' Circle and all the Berwyn book clubs, you know."

"Yes. You must have been very proud of her."

Her eyes were bright with sudden tears, but she caught herself, blinked them back, and was ready with a smile when Tim returned with the book and handed it to Jack.

Jack took it gratefully and thanked them both.

Mrs. Underwood nodded and moved away, greeting an elderly lady who had just entered the room. "Aunt Edith, how good of you to come."

"A lady," Jack said, gazing after her. "The courage shines through."

I agreed.

Harry wandered over, glad to see someone he knew. He eyed the book under Jack's arm and commented on it. "So you finally located a copy."

"Yes, Mrs. Underwood is lending me hers."

"I don't understand what happened to Marcia's. She had all her books in order, all the novels lined up alphabetically by author's name, and it should have been right there on the shelf, between Turgenev and Updike. It amused her to be traveling in such fast company. That is, eventually it amused her. When she was in the throes of writing it and getting it published, it was agony for all concerned. I don't think she ever willingly uncovered her typewriter again. Poor Marcia."

"And yet," Jack said, "she went on to become a very successful editor."

"She certainly did," Harry said, but his voice was blank, as if he had long since gone beyond approval or disapproval.

"I suppose you'll be selling her co-op apartment," I said, mostly because I was curious.

"Well, it's part of her estate," Harry said, "and therefore it will go to the boys. But the will hasn't been probated yet, and there will be some red tape. Marcia's brother, Bill, is executor, and I'm sure that everything will work out all right. Eventually, of course, the apartment will be sold. I've talked to Bill about it. We'll probably set the money aside for the boys' education."

"Hank and Tim will move in with you, then?" I was prying, I know, but Harry seemed to be perfectly willing to talk about it.

"Yes, I don't think there's any problem there." But he hesitated, a thread of doubt in his voice.

"You've straightened out everything with Captain Reilly, I understand," Jack cut in smoothly.

"I hope so," Harry replied. "A very thorough man, Captain Reilly."

Jack smiled, and I wondered how many hours of patient questioning lay behind that dry remark: a very thorough man, Captain Reilly.

I talked to the boys for a while and then Jack glanced at his watch —it was nearly five—and I took the cue. After we said our good-bys, Hank and Tim followed us to the car, to give us directions, they said, and I hugged them both and promised to see them next month in the city. They looked forlorn as we drove away, and I waved steadily until we turned the corner and they were out of sight.

It was still a gray day, though the morning drizzle had long since stopped. I had been carrying my raincoat around for hours, and I was glad to throw it on the back seat and get rid of it for a while. Turning back, I almost sat on the copy of Marcia's book, and I picked it up and looked at it curiously. *Changing Seasons: A Novel for Our Times* by Mary Marcia Underwood. The back cover was sprinkled with advance quotes, all hailing the arrival of a first-rank writer. The flap copy outlined the familiar-sounding plot and wound up with two sentences about the writer, identifying her with the time and place of the novel and hinting strongly that the book was autobiographical. But nothing at all about Marcia Richardson, short-story writer, editor, transplanted New Yorker, wife, and mother. And no picture. I suppose she'd had some vague idea that all that was irrelevant to the kind of novel she was writing.

"Want to read it?" Jack asked.

"No. I'm up to my ears in books. I don't see why you're so interested, either."

"Curiosity. I don't expect any revelations, though I suppose that's possible. It's just that the book seems to have been some kind of turning point in her life, and everyone who knew her then comments on it—Harry, her mother, her agent."

"And Rachel MacDowell, too," I said, remembering her odd comments at lunch on Wednesday. "But if it was a turning point, she made that turning ten years ago. She was murdered Monday night."

"Yes," Jack said, but his mind was on something else. "I'll be curious to see how she treats the father figure in the book. Did she ever talk about her own father?"

"No, not that I remember. He died when she was a child, you know. It was the war. Somebody told me he was killed in action—in the South Pacific, I think." Was it Tim who'd told me?

"That was a curious remark Mrs. Underwood made about the book, didn't you think?"

"That the family was all idealized except for the father. Yes, I caught that, too. Strange." I tried to tie it in, but I was groping. "Perhaps to Marcia, as a child, a father going away was a form of desertion, and it didn't really matter why he had gone. Even being a war hero wasn't a good enough reason."

Jack agreed. "Yes, and later, when she was grown up and knew better, the negative reactions from childhood were still there. Yes, that's quite possible, I suppose."

We drove along in companionable silence for a while, and I fished a map out of the glove compartment and found our route. Jack didn't seem to need any directions.

I wondered what had happened to Frank Reilly and asked about him.

"Oh, he drove down yesterday," Jack said, "and he hopes to finish up in Philadelphia today."

"That doesn't tell me much."

"He's checking out some records."

"Sure. Next thing you'll tell me is that he's following up some leads."

Jack laughed. "He's doing that, too. He may be chasing red herrings, for all I know, and dashing down blind alleys, too. This is a crazy case, Karen, but unless the murderer conveniently steps forward to confess or unless a witness tips us off, we have no choice but to cover all the ground we can."

"You don't waffle very well," I said. "You start talking in clichés and it detracts from your image. I liked it better when you were being Sincere and Open and telling me everything I might read in the newspapers."

"This case hasn't been in the papers for three days. We've been lucky."

"How about finding that body in Brooklyn? That was in the papers. Isn't that tied in?"

Jack slowed the car and turned to look at me. "What are you talking about?"

"There. I was right. It *is* tied in. Captain Frank Reilly and his no comments about the body of a young woman in the trunk of a car. In Brooklyn. What was he doing over in Brooklyn in the middle of a front-page murder in Manhattan?"

"No comment."

"That's not fair. I've told you everything I know up to now, and you've turned into a sphinx."

"I'm a cop."

"That's no excuse. I don't think I'll tell you anything else I've found out."

"Ever hear of obstruction of justice?"

52

"You'd have to subpoena me."

"Not necessarily."

"Oh, you mean that other thing: misprision of a felony. Nobody is ever convicted of that." I was sure of my grounds because I had clipped an article out of *The New York Times* and had just reread it Thursday night when I was thinking about the case.

"Good God! Misprision. What do you know about misprision? What's got into you?"

"Misprision of a felony. It means not coming forward and telling all you know about a crime."

"*I know* what misprision means, for God's sake."

"Actually, I'm not even technically guilty of that, since I don't know if what I know has any relationship at all to a crime. I mean, if I'm left completely in the dark about what is going on, how do I know if any evidence I might have is tied in?"

Jack glared at me, and I had an inspiration.

"If you only tell me what appears in the papers, I guess the thing to do is talk to this reporter I know and suggest a few questions he could ask about bodies in Brooklyn and whatnot."

"Come on, Karen, you wouldn't do a thing like that. You want to find Marcia's murderer as much as we do."

"Sure I do. But I believe in a free press, too. Maybe the reporters can help you dig up the truth. Look at Watergate."

Jack groaned. "We can't spend half our time with reporters. Be reasonable, Karen. How can I tell you everything you want to know? It's not as if we have a privileged relationship, like a lawyer and a client."

"*I know* what a privileged relationship is," I said, imitating his exasperation. "Like a priest hearing a confession. Like a doctor and a patient."

"Like a husband and a wife," Jack said. The phrase hung in the air for a minute, and he repeated it with relish: "Like a husband and a wife." And then we both laughed.

"Well, I'll keep it in mind for emergencies," Jack said. "And you won't stir up the reporters, will you, if I answer a few reasonable questions?"

"No."

"Maybe I could get you on blackmail," he mused aloud. "If I were only wired right now . . ."

"Oh, don't be an idiot. Just cooperate a little. You don't have to tell me any state secrets."

"That's good to know. I'll just pretend you're an obnoxious reporter and this is a hastily called press conference. Your move."

"OK. You can begin by telling me whether that was Shirley's body. Shirley Hastings."

"Now, why would you ever think that?"

"She's disappeared. Or at least, we can't find her. Abby—you remember Abby, don't you? You drank two cups of her coffee but you didn't know how to fix her clock radio."

Jack grinned. "Very sweet girl, Abby. A cooperative witness, too. But you were telling me about Shirley Hastings."

It occurred to me that this was a very peculiar press conference: *I* was answering all the questions. I cooperated, though; my time would come.

"Yes. Well, Shirley isn't working for that advertising agency any more," I explained. "She was probably fired. And her home phone has been disconnected. And when Abby tried to call her father in Massapequa, there was no answer. And her aunt didn't know where she was, either."

"Slow down. How did you know she came from Massapequa? Abby didn't say anything about that Thursday."

"She didn't know then. We did a little investigating. . . . No, that's not the right expression. We were checking out some records and following up a lead."

"Come on, Karen, I'm playing along with this charade, but you have to cooperate, too."

"I *am* cooperating. I'm just pulling your leg a little, too. Anyway, Abby has a friend in the personnel department at Berwyn and she looked up the records. Didn't you know she was from Massapequa?"

"Yes. The records *I* checked out were at the advertising agency. And you're right. She *had* been fired. They couldn't understand her. She had been doing a fine job for three months, and then, almost deliberately, she began making mistakes, failing to show up on time, or even failing to come in at all. It was almost as if she were asking to be fired. Why would she do that?"

"I don't know. Maybe she wanted to be fired so she could start collecting unemployment right away."

"Hey, maybe you've got something there. Write it down. I'll check out claims on Monday. What else?"

"What do you mean, what else? I still don't have an answer about that body in Brooklyn."

"Still unidentified."

"Why didn't you ask Ricardo when you arrested him?"

There was a long pause, and then Jack's voice came out, deceptively calm. "Karen, what makes you think we arrested Ricardo?"

"No. My question first. Why didn't you ask him?"

Jack drove in silence for a few minutes before he answered. "We did ask Ricardo, but he couldn't make an identification. The face—well, it was pretty battered. Ricardo nearly fainted when we took him to the morgue. He said he couldn't tell if it was Shirley or not."

"What about the clothes? Or any identifying marks?"

"Blue jeans and a T-shirt. Pretty anonymous. And they didn't fit the body, either. And Ricardo was so shaken that he was almost incoherent after that. He had been so cocky up to then. Claimed he hadn't seen Shirley for two months. By the way, she was not on drugs, according to him. And that body in Brooklyn—no drugs there, either. Ricardo may be a major dealer, but it doesn't follow that he's a user, and it doesn't follow that he turned her on, either. He just didn't talk about her that way. He thought she was pretty, entertaining, kooky. Actually, he had a wonderful Spanish word for her: *despalomada*. Pigeon-brained. Scatter-brained, I guess we'd say."

"So why did they break up?"

"Ricardo wasn't very clear about that. I think it was *her* idea, but he wouldn't admit that. Wounded pride. *Muy macho,* these Latins. A terrible affront for a woman to walk out on you."

"And it was after that that Shirley changed at the agency? Arranged to get herself fired?"

"That seems to be the timing, yes." Jack looked over at me. "So what does that suggest to you?"

"I'm not sure. That Shirley was ready to make some kind of change in her life. Broke up with a guy, got out of a job, cleared out of her apartment. That is, I don't know that she cleared out, but she had her phone disconnected."

"She moved out two weeks ago. Not that there was that much moving to do; it was a furnished place and she simply packed up her personal stuff and drove off in a car. The neighbors don't know any more than that."

"I see. Are you still holding Ricardo?"

"No. He made bail next day. The feds weren't too happy about our taking him in. He'd been under observation for quite a while and the case against him is still building. Now tell me how you knew we picked him up."

"Oh, well, I just happened to be in the neighborhood, on Madison Avenue, when you arrested him. Anybody might have seen it."

"Sure. Anybody. Where were you? Staked out in a tree or something?"

"No, I just happened to be having a cup of coffee in a little restaurant across the street. Anybody could have been there."

"Amazing coincidence. Karen, this isn't a game, you know. Somebody like Ricardo plays for keeps. Marcia was murdered. And we still don't know if that is Shirley's body. You stay out of this."

"Believe me, I have no desire to get into the front lines. I can't begin to figure out what's going on, and I don't really see the connection between Marcia's murder and Shirley's disappearance. Or maybe her murder. Was she killed?"

"We don't know yet if that is Shirley's body, remember. But yes, that young woman, whoever she was, was killed. Shot through the head. The face was battered afterwards—to prevent identification, I assume. The fingerprints aren't on record."

"So you'll have to go by her dental records."

"You read too many mysteries."

"Well, won't you?"

"Her dental charts would be very helpful, yes. You wouldn't happen to know who Shirley's dentist is, by any chance?"

"No, I don't know who Shirley's dentist is by any chance. And I doubt if Abby does, either."

"Her parents would know, but they're off on vacation, touring Canada, according to the neighbors."

56

"Yes, I know. Her aunt got a card from the Gaspé Peninsula."

"All right, I give up. How do you know her aunt?"

"Why, of course! Her aunt! *She* might know who Shirley's dentist is. Mrs. Dimaria. There can't be too many Dimarias in Massapequa. You can check it out. And the neighbors might know. I promise not to make a single phone call. There, you see? I've given you a terrific lead."

"Write it down," Jack said shortly. "And would you be so kind as to tell me how you know that Shirley has an aunt named Mrs. Dimaria?"

"Didn't I tell you? When Abby got the records from personnel, I had her call the Hastingses' number in Massapequa."

"I called it, too, but there's no answer. The family is in Canada, remember?"

"Sure. But Abby didn't know that when she phoned, so she just kept calling all day, and the next morning, too. And that's when Mrs. Dimaria answered. She just happened to be there to water the plants and see if the house was all right and everything. So she must live pretty close, don't you think? She wouldn't be driving all the way out from the city just to do that."

"It's a strong possibility. And you think she might know who Shirley's dentist is?"

"Well, why not? She knows the family that well. She's *part* of the family, for heaven's sake. She probably has discussed dentists at some time or another with Shirley's mother. I bet they're sisters. It's worth a call, don't you think?"

"Yes, you're right. It's worth a call."

"But I still don't see a connection with Marcia's murder."

"To tell you the truth, I don't either."

"Every theory I have seems so far-fetched," I went on.

"Tell me a few. Maybe you'll hit on something."

He probably thought he was diverting me from asking questions, but I didn't mind. I'd get back to that later. We still had at least an hour's drive ahead of us, and maybe we would stop for dinner, too. I was certainly getting hungry. Lunch had been a very hasty affair because Joe had been running late and we had only had time to stop at a drive-in for hamburgers.

57

"Theories," I said, gathering my thoughts. "Well, this is going to sound silly because I don't really believe it myself. But suppose Shirley was really shaken when Marcia fired her. And she brooded over it. And then when she was breaking up with Ricardo, she said something about it. And Ricardo got it into his head that Marcia was to blame for Shirley's leaving him. So he went after her."

"Two months after he heard about it from Shirley?"

"We only have Ricardo's word on the timing."

"And he shot her with her own gun?"

"Well, maybe he took his gun along, but when he saw hers, he grabbed it from her and shot her with it."

"Twice."

"Well, why not? Somebody shot her twice, whoever it was. Maybe the murderer shot her with his own gun, then used Marcia's afterward, to fire the second shot."

"Two shots had been fired from Marcia's gun."

"Oh, *I* don't know. I'm making this up as I go along. Maybe she fired at him and he fired at her. And then he fired her own gun the second time, to cover up the ballistics mark of the first shot, or something."

Jack sighed. "And what happened to the bullet she fired?"

"She hit him!" I said triumphantly. "All you have to do is find somebody who is walking around with a bullet in him."

"Great. All right. Any other theories?"

"We could try to work out something about Shirley's dental records and the fact that Harry Richardson is a dentist. . . . You don't like that? Well, give me two minutes to dream up something else."

"I'll wait. And while I'm waiting, what do you say to stopping somewhere for dinner?"

Abby was right, our minds *do* work alike. But all I said was, "Fine, I'm ravenous."

"So am I. Do you think you can hold out until Fort Lee? I know a pretty fair Italian restaurant there, not far from the George Washington Bridge."

"Sounds good. I wonder if it's the same one Elly talks about."

"Elly?"

"Elly Crawford. My friend who lives upstairs. The one I went to the movies with Tuesday."

"Oh, sure, Elly."

I went back to concocting another theory about why Ricardo could have killed Marcia. She wasn't on drugs, so it couldn't be that she owed him money or anything like that. Maybe he was tied in with that slimy lawyer Ted Ferris. Which reminded me, I hadn't asked Jack what had happened to him. I proceeded to do so.

"What happened to him? He's up on Cape Cod, according to his secretary. He'll be back Monday and I'm going to see him then. Why?"

"I'm still trying to work out a connection between Marcia and Shirley and Ricardo, and I thought I'd try to fit Ted Ferris in, too."

"Any luck?"

"This is going to be even crazier than my other theory."

"I'm listening."

"This time it's Ted Ferris who shoots her. He thought she was pestering him to marry her or something. No, that's not the way Marcia would react. Still, maybe it's what Ferris would think if she phoned him. So he goes to see her, and it's the same business about the guns. He has a twenty-two, too, and she gets off one shot and hits him. You must be sure to look on Monday, to see if he's concealing a gunshot wound."

"Do you want to make a note of it?"

"I know. I told you that this would be silly. Anyway, Ferris shoots her and drives back to Cape Cod and nobody realizes he was away. The whole business with Ricardo and Shirley has nothing to do with anything. That's not even Shirley in the morgue. She's driving around Canada with her parents. What do you think?"

"I like the happy ending. But what about the poor girl in the morgue?"

"That can be anybody. Aren't there a lot of people who run away? Somebody underground from the Weathermen or somebody reported missing?"

"Actually, of course, that's a very strong possibility, and we're working on it. There are thousands of runaways every year. This is,

59

truly, a case where we are checking through the records, even if we haven't come across a promising lead yet."

"Will you tell me if you find out who it is?"

"Yes, that would be in the papers. I'll let you know. There's one thing you've left out of your theories, Karen—the missing book."

"I don't see why you keep harping on that. What would the murderer want with her old novel?"

"I haven't the faintest idea. But I find it very strange that it disappeared, and it's not the kind of coincidence that I believe in."

"It doesn't make any sense. Taking the book away just calls attention to it. If there *is* something in it that's in any way incriminating, now you'll look for it and find it. If it was just there on the shelf, who would have paid any attention to it?"

"Unless we are *supposed* to be diverted into looking at it closely," Jack said, half to himself. "Well, I'll read it tomorrow and see."

"What a twisted mind the murderer must have," I said, "and cool too, if he deliberately went over to the bookshelves afterward and stole a book to mislead you."

"Yes, you'd think if he wanted to call attention to it, he'd have swept a shelf of books to the floor to make sure we'd notice."

"And if he didn't want you to pay attention, then he could have just spread out the books a little so you wouldn't see the gap where one had been taken away. Sometimes I do that when I lend books."

"There's always the possibility, of course, that Marcia had pulled out the book herself and lent it to somebody to read. I may be making too much of the whole thing."

That's what I had thought all along, but I saw no reason to say it again. I remembered, though, that I hadn't finished asking him questions, so I picked up on that. "Did you talk to everybody in the apartment building?"

"Frank handled most of that. Nobody heard a thing. Understandable, actually. The walls are thick, the air-conditioners were on, and a twenty-two doesn't make all that much noise."

"And I gathered from the papers that the doorman is new and doesn't know the people yet."

"Right. That was a particularly bad break. It's possible that when we finally locate the murderer, the doorman might remember seeing him, but I don't put much faith in that."

"What about the doorman who was there before?"

"What about him?"

"Well, he might have had a grudge against Marcia if she was instrumental in having him fired."

"No. She wasn't the only one who complained about his drunkenness, if that's what you mean. The building management does the hiring and firing, and her name wasn't mentioned when they let the old guy go. Frank looked him up, just to keep things tidy, and he was with some pals up in the Bronx the night of the murder."

"I see. So what it means is that practically anybody could have visited Marcia that night and could have come and gone unrecognized."

"Right."

"And since she was killed with her own gun, chances are that the crime wasn't planned ahead."

"Yes," Jack agreed. "Unless we go back to your fanciful theories about three shots."

"Well, then, it seems to me that the whole thing is wide open. You can hardly eliminate anyone. Anyone could have gone in, anyone could have used the gun, and it could have happened practically any time Monday night, although I still think that the timing of my phone calls was significant."

"So do I," Jack said. "And it's also significant that we can't find out who Marcia was talking to at nine o'clock, any more than we can find out who took the book from the shelf. If the call was innocent, or the book had actually been lent by Marcia, we should have found out by now. My hunch is that the book and the call and the murder are all connected. And since she has an unlisted phone, it argues that the caller knew her rather well."

"Of course, she might have made the call herself."

"Yes."

"Wouldn't it be strange if she had just been calling to get the weather report or something simple like that? Or calling somebody who wasn't home, so the phone just rang and rang?"

"The problem is that we can hardly rule anything out at this stage," Jack said.

61

I mulled that over for a while and made a mental list of everyone under suspicion. There was Joe Blackwell, managing editor of RC. I couldn't believe Joe could commit murder, but there was no doubt that he was next in line for Marcia's job and probably needed the money that would go with the promotion. I knew his wife Dotty had inherited something from her father—how else could they afford to live in Manhattan and keep the kids in private school?—but Joe inevitably needed more. Even taking Terry to Hungarian restaurants must have cost something.

And there was Ricardo, somehow involved in the drug traffic and obviously of a more violent temper than anybody else connected with the case. I couldn't imagine what his motives could be, but if his pride had really been wounded when Shirley Hastings walked out on him, who knew what direction his rage might have taken.

And what about Shirley herself? She was the one who had actually been fired by Marcia. That was hardly a reason to kill, but she was a strange kid, and this sudden disappearance might have been planned.

There was Harry, Marcia's former husband. When two people had been married for sixteen years and then divorced for two, there must have been all sorts of problems buried beneath the surface. Maybe he was tired of paying out child support. Maybe he wanted the boys to live with him. He wasn't inheriting any of Marcia's money directly (Berwyn has fairly generous life-insurance policies on editors in Marcia's bracket), but the boys would get the bulk of it, and so he, Harry, stood to benefit indirectly.

Then there was Ted Ferris, the lawyer. I had never met him, but he sounded repulsive from Meredith's description. And there was something sleazy about him and the way he moved in on his vulnerable divorce clients. He was by far my favorite candidate.

Anyone else? I ruled out Meredith Baker, the agent. She was a gossip and a busybody, but she seemed genuinely fond of Marcia. Rachel MacDowell, the editor of Biography Book Club, was a very distant possibility. She hadn't much liked having Shirley fired, I guess, and perhaps it was something of a blow to her pride to be sharing a secretary now instead of having one all to herself, but that wasn't grounds for murder. And she had been a little strange at lunch on

Wednesday, but then we had all been on edge that day.

I searched for additional suspects. There was X, who phoned Marcia and stole her book, but I couldn't get a handle on him—or her—at all.

"Have you figured it out yet?" Jack asked, reading my mind.

"No. I don't like anybody for the role except Ted Ferris, and he's the only one I don't know. I keep thinking there's somebody else whose name hasn't come into this yet."

"So do I," Jack said. "And I don't think we've exhausted the possibilities of all those people in publishing. Tell me how you operate on a day-by-day basis. No, first tell me about the president of your division. What's his name again?"

"George T. Griffith."

"Right. Griffith. He struck me as a pretty cold fish. What's he like?"

"Oh, he's a numbers man, came up through the accounting route. And he was wished on Berwyn Publishing Company by Phoenix Industries after the takeover a few years ago. He had been in mail-order seeds and gardening equipment at Phoenix, turned the division around and made it profitable, so the story goes. So he came to Berwyn Book Clubs; it's mail order, too, you see, and on a corporate level nobody knows gardens from books. It's all 'product' to be sold."

"I see. It doesn't sound as if your Mr. Griffith got a hearty welcome when he came."

"That was two years before I joined the clubs, so I don't speak from firsthand experience, but you're probably right. George came in as business manager and vice president of the division, and he got the president's job about two and a half years ago, just six months after I was hired. But I was a pretty small fish in those days, not a club editor yet. I'm still a pretty small fish, come to think of it. Anyway, I didn't know the politics of the situation."

"And now you do?"

"Well, to a degree. George reorganized the whole structure from top to bottom, set up different lines of authority, stepped on a lot of toes. Actually, I suppose the editorial department was less affected than the rest of the division. Marcia was already editorial director and Joe was managing editor, and he didn't really mess around with us very much. He doesn't seem to understand the editorial process at all, which most of the time is just fine. It means he leaves us alone on a day-to-day basis.

"On the other hand, it also means he can send out the damnedest memos, outlining impossible operating procedures. If we tried to follow them literally, we'd be so tied up in red tape we'd never meet our deadlines. Marcia was always terrific at clearing up messes like that, though. She'd summon up all her charm, go into his office, and explain the situation to him. And she usually had a draft of a revised memo with her, and he'd approve it on the spot. The postscript memo, we called it. Nobody ever pays any attention to George's first memo on editorial operations for at least three days. We always wait that long to see if there's a follow-up."

"He sounds pretty useless."

"Well, he's done some good things, in the areas of the business he knows something about. He got the whole computer mess straightened out. He started that while he was business manager. We now get accurate sales figures, and we know the profit margin on everything down to the last penny, or at any rate we're supposed to, if the programmers keep up to date with the price changes. It makes a big difference in the way we operate. I took over MSI just two years ago, when the computer shift was going through, and I don't know how I could have run things under the old system."

"So on balance he's all right."

"Could be worse. Could be better, too. He procrastinates on some things. I don't know how long he's going to keep Joe Blackwell dangling before he decides to promote him." I explained Joe's current problems, in which he had most of Marcia's responsibilities and almost none of her authority.

"Will Joe be able to handle the promotion if he gets it?" Jack asked.

"I think so. Certainly better than anybody else in the department. I don't know how well he'll get along with George, though. I'm not sure he's got Marcia's tact on handling postscript memos, for instance."

"I see. So George might be looking around for somebody from outside."

"That's a gloomy thought, but he could be."

"I wonder if George has mentioned that possibility to anyone else."

64

"I don't know. Since Marcia's death, I suppose there have been some feelers out to see who might be good in the job."

"No, I mean before Marcia's death," Jack said.

"I don't understand you," I said. "Before Marcia's death he wasn't looking to replace her. I think he was happy with her in the job."

"I'm not suggesting he wasn't. I mean he might have been having lunch with one of his publishing friends. . . . Does he have publishing friends, by the way, or is he always with the money men?"

"He knows people in publishing, if that's what you mean. Through Marcia, mostly. She took him along on business lunches sometimes if there was someone he wanted to meet. Or if someone from one of the publishing houses expressed an interest in meeting him—someone on a high enough level, that is."

"So he knows important people in publishing."

"Yes, sure."

"Well, suppose he was having lunch with one of them, and they got to discussing which editors were good at their jobs, who was a real comer, that sort of thing."

I couldn't see George doing that, but I let it pass. Instead I said, "I don't see what you're driving at."

"All right, look at it this way. Somehow George hears that there is this terrific editor out there. John Terrific, his name is."

"I'd like to meet him," I said. "Is he single?"

"Don't distract me. I'm building a theory I like better than yours —that third-bullet nonsense."

"OK. I'll play. George hears about this great editor John Terrific."

"Yes. And on some occasion when George is talking about possible changes in your department, someone asks him what he would do if he had to replace Marcia. There ought to be a contingency plan, right?"

"I guess so."

"So George says he's got a pretty good managing editor in Joe Blackwell, but maybe Joe isn't ready for anything bigger right now. However, George has heard that John Terrific is the brightest light on the publishing scene."

"And where does that lead us?" I asked.

"Why, don't you see? The word of this gets back to John Terrific, who is feeling stifled and unappreciated where he is, and he thinks that if only Marcia were out of the way . . ."

"I like the third-bullet theory better."

"Maybe we can incorporate the two. When I find Terrific, I'll know he's guilty when I dig the twenty-two slug out of his forearm."

"But really, though—" I was trying to treat it all seriously—"how would you follow up on a theory like that?"

"I'm going to see George Griffith again on Monday. I'll ask him how he's proceeding in his job search."

"He'll smother you in words and won't tell you a thing."

"I'll appeal to him as a great mind who can help the police unravel a baffling case. You'd be surprised at how many grown men fancy themselves as great detectives. Grown women, too," he added. "Stake-outs in a coffee shop and that sort of thing."

He had me there, but only temporarily. "You didn't explain why John Terrific stole Marcia's book," I said.

"Details. I haven't figured out that part yet. Maybe he'll explain that when he blurts out his guilt. It's always so convenient on television when the murderer tells all just before the final commercial. The only confessions *we* get come from cranks who are willing to confess to anything."

"You mean there's been a confession in this case?"

"Three so far. You list a special phone number to call and the weirdos come out of the woodwork."

"Don't you follow up on confessions?"

"I don't personally, no. But there are detectives out beating the bushes on this case, turning up all kinds of freaks. We compare notes constantly. I'm holding a special brief for the publishing world, though. I think that's where we'll find the perpetrator, as the jargon goes."

"You ought to come to the memorial service for Marcia, then. The place will be swarming with publishing types."

"Yes, I've made a note of it. Thursday. We really should crack the case next week, with any luck at all."

We had reached Fort Lee by then, and I could see the bridge in the distance, a necklace of twinkling lights strung out between the tall towers. Beyond was Manhattan and, as always, I felt that special lift, that radiation of excitement New York still holds for me. Utterly irrational. I had learned to bad-mouth the place, like every other New Yorker, transplanted or native, but I still can't imagine myself anywhere else.

Jack found the side street he was looking for and pulled up beside the restaurant in a perfectly legitimate parking space. Inside we were greeted effusively in a mixture of Italian and English and seated at a table for two that could easily have accommodated six.

I commented on the size, and Jack said that they'd probably bring us enough food for six, too, so all that space would not go to waste. I could have made a meal on the antipasto alone, but I saved some room for the scampi and was on my third glass of Chianti, listening all the while to some long, involved explanation from Jack about how he had found this place and how the owner's wife was related to somebody he knew in Woodside, Queens, just a few blocks from where he lived in Jackson Heights.

For some reason, that reminded me of my first day in New York, six years ago, when I was walking down Fifth Avenue and ran into my high-school gym teacher from Neenah, Wisconsin. She was carrying a tennis racket, and we said hello to each other as if it were the most natural thing in the world. And then she asked me where she could find a place to have it restrung, but I didn't know. And we parted and I haven't seen her since. There had seemed to be some point to the story when I started it, but I couldn't remember what it was. So we looked at each other a bit uncertainly and laughed some more.

I said no to another glass of wine, and Jack said that was good because we had finished the bottle and it was a good thing I wasn't driving. He ordered coffee and zabaglione, and I didn't see how I'd swallow anything else at all, but I did and it was delicious.

We were still lingering over coffee when a familiar face emerged from the haze, and there was Elly Crawford hovering over us, accompanied by her boy friend, Eddy Palmieri.

"I thought it was you," Elly said, and I proceeded to make introductions.

"We just came for coffee and dessert," Elly said, and Eddy signaled the waiter, who brought two chairs to our table so they could join us.

I didn't think we had asked them, but it seemed to be a *fait accompli.*
The pastry cart appeared as if by magic, and Eddy and Elly made their
selections, two apiece. The waiter poured coffee for them and refilled
our cups, and there we were, trapped.

"We come here all the time," Eddy said. "My uncle owns this place,
and he keeps wanting me to join him in the business."

Jack made some kind of polite sound, but his heart wasn't in it.

"I haven't made up my mind yet," Eddy went on. "I'm still convinced I can make it as an actor."

"He was in a revival of *The Master Builder* last year," Elly said
helpfully. "Maybe you saw it? Very original staging, in a warehouse.
All in black and white, like an old print."

Jack said he had missed it. I had, too. I made a rule for Elly once:
I would only go to something Off-Broadway if it had been running
three weeks. Off-Off-Broadway, six weeks. So far I had been caught
only once.

"It was reviewed in *Cue,*" Elly said, "but everybody else ignored
it. The establishment is so unfair to young talent and new ideas, don't
you think?"

Jack evaded the question and said it was probably hard to break in.

"That's just what I mean," Elly said. "Three years, and my name
still hasn't been in *The New York Times.* Or Eddy's, either."

"I'm thinking of changing mine for the stage," Eddy said. "Nobody
knows how to pronounce Palmieri. I think Eddy Palmer has a nice
ring to it. Or maybe Edward Palmer. What do you think?"

Jack stole a glance at me, but I was managing to keep a straight
face.

"I think it depends on what kind of image you are trying to project," Jack said.

"Of course, the image," Eddy agreed. "Eddy is kind of young,
devil-may-care. Edward is more serious, for the classic roles."

Elly nodded in agreement. "I think names are fascinating," she
said, turning to Jack. "But I'm afraid I didn't quite catch yours."

There was a fractional pause, as if he were considering an alias, but
he said it straight, without title: Jack Morrison.

Elly's face lit up in sudden recognition. "Of course. Lieutenant Jack
Morrison. The murder case. Eddy, this is the detective I told you

about, the one investigating the murder of that editor."

Eddy looked at Jack with renewed interest, and Elly was off on one of her wild rambles. "Did Karen tell you my theory, Jack?"

Jack looked at me and I shrugged helplessly.

Elly seemed disappointed. "I figured it out right away. Her husband did it. The way I see it is that this man—he's a dentist, Eddy, but I don't remember his name . . ."

"Harry Richardson," I said. There didn't seem to be any way to stop her.

"Yes, Harry," Elly went on. "He's got plenty of motives—tired of paying for the kids, wanting them to move in with him. And maybe there's some money the kids would inherit, too. I hadn't thought of that." She looked hopefully at Jack, but he didn't comment.

"Anyway, this Harry would know how to get into the apartment without being seen. He used to live there," she explained to Eddy. "But I think what would really prove it would be finding his girl friend."

"*Cherchez la femme,*" Eddy put in wisely. "That means to look for the woman."

I had resisted looking at Jack, but I risked a brief glance. His eyes were focused on some distant area of the ceiling and his face was carefully blank.

"The way I see it," Elly went on relentlessly, "is that Harry's girl friend, whoever she is, egged him on. Like Lady Macbeth. And maybe she even fired the second shot from the gun. So they would both be guilty, of course. Kind of noble of her, in a way."

Eddy nodded in agreement. "Look for the woman," he repeated with satisfaction.

"Have you found her yet?" Elly asked Jack.

"I'm sorry," Jack said. "I can't discuss a case while we're working on it. We're checking out all the evidence, though, and there are several promising leads." He sounded convincing.

"If we only knew their signs," Elly said.

Jack looked at her as if she had come from another planet.

"Their birth signs. It's always seemed to me that the police should have an astrology expert on the staff. He could save everybody a lot of time, finding out who is compatible, who would give way to murderous rage, everything. I'm not saying that he could find the murderer in every case, of course. I'm not superstitious like that. But he, or she, could give you some valuable tips and point you in the right direction a lot of times. Don't you think that would be a good idea, Jack?"

"I doubt if the budget would stretch to cover it," Jack said dryly.

Elly shook her head. "It's just like we were saying earlier. The establishment never responds to fresh ideas. The police department is probably just as rigid as *The New York Times,* wouldn't you say so?"

"Easily," Jack agreed.

"You're different, though," Elly said. "I tell you what. You find out Marcia's birth date. And Harry's. And his girl friend's. And I have this friend who casts horoscopes, and she'll be able to tell you in a minute if you're on the right track. What do you say?"

"Well, it's an idea," Jack said diplomatically. "And now—" he looked over at me, and I nodded—"I think we'd better be heading home."

"The waiter won't charge you for Elly and me," Eddy said when Jack got the bill. "We can come here free."

Neither of us knew how to respond to that, so we let it pass in silence. Jack slid some bills under his saucer for a tip, and I said our proper good-bys while he paid the cashier.

It was cool outside and I was glad to breathe fresh air.

"Let's walk over to the lookout point," Jack suggested, and I agreed. He glanced back at the restaurant, somewhat ruefully. "I hope I don't run into them every time I go back."

"I'm sorry."

"Not your fault."

"I'm sorry anyway. It's a good place, and I'd hate to think it's spoiled for you now. And thank you. It was a terrific meal."

"I'm glad you liked it," Jack said, and his voice brightened. "You see, they've got this terrific chef, Chef John Terrific, his name is, only he wants to open his own restaurant because he's feeling stifled and unappreciated where he is now. And at lunch one day he heard there would be a chance at running a great new restaurant, if only the manager disappeared. . . ."

"Successful businesses are all alike," I said. "Every unsuccessful business fails in its own way."

"Not bad," Jack allowed, taking my hand.

We reached the lookout point, and there were half a dozen other people there admiring the view, too.

The drizzle, the clouds had all cleared away, and from this distance Manhattan looked newly washed, clean and resplendent and sparkling. Even the air was soft and sweet.

"It's just what I've always said." The voice came from an elderly man who probably thought his wife was as hard of hearing as he obviously was. "I've always said that the best thing about New Jersey is the view you have of New York." He looked around challengingly, but nobody was ready to disturb the peaceful night by arguing over that old cliché. And for all I know, everybody there believed it. I certainly did.

Jack and I walked back to the car, hand in hand, in silence, and the moment was too fragile to disturb.

We were in the car, crossing the bridge, with all Manhattan glittering ahead of us, when I understood something that had puzzled me all along.

"I know why you're a cop, Jack."

"I told you why. I was losing my student deferment and—"

"That was eleven years ago. I mean now. You're a cop because you love this city and you want to protect her."

"What a crazy romantic you are."

"No, I'm right. You're still an idealist, and you're out to set things straight."

"Well, I'd rather be a cop than a robber, if that's what you mean. It's more respectable. And better paid in the long run, too. Do you know I could retire at half salary in another nine years if I wanted to?"

"Good fringe benefits in your line of work."

"Sure. Healthy job. Takes me out of doors. Gives me a chance to meet a lot of people. Better than pushing papers all day, although God knows we do plenty of that, too."

"You love it."

71

"Yes, I love it," he said flatly. "And I even think it's worthwhile. I don't *want* mere anarchy loosed upon the world."

"Things fall apart, the center will not hold. . . ."

"I'm holding. I don't see why good men should lack all conviction. Or good women, either. I think the world is worth saving." His voice turned mocking, self-mocking. "That's the inspiration speech, suitable for Boy Scout lectures."

He didn't fool me for a minute. "I bet you're the only man on the police force who goes around quoting Yeats."

"Not quite. Anyway, the deputy chief inspector unreels Shakespeare by the yard on every conceivable occasion. Before I met Mike I never realized there was so much sex and violence in all those plays."

"Look at Elly tonight with that Lady Macbeth stuff."

"Oh, Elly." He shook his head. "For a minute there I was afraid she had gone out playing detective, too."

"You mean there's something to that story? That Harry has a girl who might have egged him on to murder?"

"You put things so baldly."

"I'm still the reporter at the press conference."

"Yes. Well, you were doing a little of that with Harry this afternoon at Mrs. Underwood's. Did you realize that?"

"You mean when I asked whether he would get custody of the boys. Yes, I knew I was prying. But I wanted to know, and he wasn't unwilling to talk about it. It's only natural to wonder about things like that. It's what everybody has been speculating about. I'm sure it's one of the things your Captain Reilly asked him about right away."

"I'm sure it was, too, with all the follow-up questions about selling off the co-op apartment and settling the will and talking about where they would all be living in the future. But when you started off on that same line of inquiry, right after the funeral . . . I could see that Harry would wind up being terribly embarrassed. He wouldn't really choose to announce his plans to marry a second time on the day of his first wife's funeral."

"I didn't know he was getting married again."

"Yes, well, you would have had it out of him in another two minutes. And he hasn't told his children yet."

"I didn't know. He wouldn't have had to tell me. I don't see why you're blaming me for something I didn't even do."

"I don't want to blame you for anything. I'm just telling you you ought to know better than . . . Oh, forget it. There was no harm done."

What a dumb thing for him to get angry about. And he still hadn't explained about Harry's new girl friend. He was always going off on tangents just when we got to something really interesting. Well, he might as well get truly mad at me, because I was curious, and I meant to push right ahead.

"Who is the girl friend?" I asked.

"God, you're persistent."

"I think I said that to you once, too. Who's the girl friend?"

"Jean Ann Larrabee," he said shortly. And he avoided the follow-up questions by following through himself. "I don't know how he met her. She teaches home economics in Riverdale, she's about thirty, and she hasn't been married before. OK?"

"OK. When are they getting married?"

"At this point, they don't know. They had been talking about next month, but that was before Marcia was killed, before they knew they would be having the boys live with them. Now they're holding off until Tim and Hank get to know her a little, so that there can be some kind of adjustment."

"I see. And nobody in Marcia's family knows yet? Her mother or her brother or anybody?"

"No. Harry was going to tell Marcia the next time he saw her, but there wasn't a next time."

"I wonder . . ."

We were almost home, pulling around the corner into 87th Street, stopping in the no-parking zone.

Jack switched off the ignition and turned to look at me again. "*Now* what is it?"

"Oh, I don't know."

"Come on. You've got another wild theory inside, kicking and screaming to get out. Give."

"All right, if you insist. Want to come up for coffee?"

"No. Just tell me."

So he was really angry. "It's not important. I was just thinking that it might have been Harry who phoned her at nine o'clock Monday

73

night and he told her about getting married again. And she was feeling kind of shaken by that since it came so soon after the break-up with that sleazy lawyer. And that's why she had the gun out of the drawer."

"I see. God, what a messy case this is. But do you really think that Marcia might have wanted to take her own life?"

"I wouldn't have thought so before. Now I just don't know."

"Karen, I want you to promise me something."

"I'm listening."

"Please don't discuss all this with Elly or Abby or Joe or Mrs. Dimaria or anybody else. Do you promise?"

"Yes."

"I should never have told you . . . anything."

So that's what was eating him. He was having second thoughts about having unbent and acted human for a change. And all that stuff about my talking so much was really directed at himself. A pure case of projection.

I slammed the car door behind me, and then I heard his door open and close and he followed me to the house.

"I just wanted to make sure you didn't get mugged before you got inside."

"Sure. Thanks." I unlocked the door and he stepped back two paces. Did he think I was going to attack or something? "Good night, Jack. It was certainly an interesting day."

A smile broke through. "I have to agree with you there. Good night, Karen."

I heard my phone ringing before I got the front door open. Who could be calling at 11:30 on a Saturday night?

Meredith Baker, that's who, and she sounded distraught. "Karen, at last! Are you all right?"

"Sure, Meredith. What's the matter?"

"But, my dear, I have been trying to reach you for hours. We've all been so worried. I called the Blackwells five times to tell them you still weren't home. Where were you? Were you with Lieutenant Morrison the whole time? Did he take you to the police station? Karen, what happened?"

"Nothing, Meredith. It's all right. Everything is all right. We stopped for dinner on the way home. That's all. And we ran into some friends. And he brought me home. I don't see why you're so worked up."

"But, my dear, to leave a funeral in the company of a policeman! I thought he might have arrested you. You're always entitled to make a telephone call, Karen. Did you know that?"

"Yes, Meredith. But I wasn't arrested."

"Joe kept telling me not to worry," Meredith said. "But he was really getting concerned the last time I called him."

I bet, I thought. He was wondering if he'd have to shut off his phone to get an uninterrupted night's sleep.

"I'll call him now and tell him you're home safely," Meredith said. "Or maybe you should call him, dear, so he can hear the sound of your voice."

"No, Meredith, I don't want to bother him. Did you have a good trip back?"

"Yes. Joe dropped me off right in front of my building. Wasn't that nice of him? It was barely six thirty. That was more than five hours ago, Karen."

"Yes. Well, I'm sorry you were worried, but I'm really all right."

"And he didn't arrest you?"

"Not even once."

"Did he make a pass at you?"

"Oh, Meredith, for heaven's sake."

"Did he?"

"No! We went to the Underwoods', we drove home, we stopped for dinner. Don't make such a fuss."

"Well, I just wanted you to know that we were concerned about you. We talked of nothing else the whole ride home."

That must have been a jolly trip. I bet Dotty was ready to jump down her throat. Or maybe she just detached herself from the whole situation and let Joe bear the brunt of it.

For the nth time I assured Meredith I was all right, and she finally let me hang up.

Did he make a pass at me! Good grief, what's the matter with her? Well, what's the matter with him?

Or, possibly, what's the matter with me?

That's a miserable train of thought.

I sat down and opened the mail and chucked it all in the wastebasket except for the Con Ed bill. The rates had gone up again, and my air-conditioner was eating up the kilowatts as if I had all the oil in Saudi Arabia at my beck and call. Maybe I did. Anyway, I wrote out a check and looked at the anemic balance left in my account.

I wondered what the city of New York paid its police lieutenants.

✦✦✦✦✦✦✦

5

✦✦✦✦✦✦✦

Monday morning I was due in an agency review meeting at ten o'clock, and Abby was so busy pulling out advertising and sales records for me that we barely had time to talk about the events of the weekend. I told her that nothing much had happened at the funeral, and I downplayed the fact that Jack had driven me home. I wouldn't have mentioned it at all, but Joe Blackwell dropped by to say that Meredith had called him at midnight Saturday just to tell him I was safe. He rolled his eyes, but he was really more interested in complaining about her extended monologues than in anything that might have happened to me.

And then he got right down to business. In the past, Marcia had always come to agency review sessions with the club editors, but Joe would be filling in for her today, and he wanted a quick briefing on Mystery, Suspense, and Intrigue.

We have agency reviews for each club twice a year, and it is the editor's primary contact with the advertising agency handling the club account. Each of the Berwyn book clubs is represented by a different advertising agency, chosen by the club's marketing director, who works closely with the agency in developing campaigns. Marketing directors and editors don't necessarily see eye to eye on advertising, and this is the source of a good deal of friction within the book-club division.

In the two years that I have been editor of MSI, three marketing directors have come and gone, and in Leroy Langner I am working with my fourth. The trouble is that a newly hired marketing director is likely to be started off with MSI and the Sports Book Club, both of them, maybe on the theory that these are going operations and somebody new couldn't foul up the procedures beyond redemption. (The first one tried, but Jerry helped me put the skids under him, and he left for greener pastures elsewhere, selling beauty kits in a franchise operation.)

The second marketing director, Anya Rosoff, was pretty good, but she didn't last long because she was just marking time until she was cleared for a job with the CIA. Really! She had fluent Russian (she claimed to be related to a cousin of the last czar), and she had her master's in business administration from Wharton. With those credentials she thought she would be invaluable figuring out Soviet five-year plans, or something. Whatever it was, she sold the CIA on the idea of hiring her, and now she spends her time reading Russian trade journals down in Langley, Virginia, and plotting graphs and making charts and writing memos. Maybe she has been instrumental in preventing stupid wheat deals, for all I know, or she has been able to size up the true production levels of ball bearings and atomic-powered widgets.

Anya was succeeded by Nate Meyer, who was obnoxious but bright. Nate was promoted and is now marketing director of Readers' Circle, and therefore he is Joe's headache, not Jerry's and mine.

But back to Leroy Langner. As marketing director of MSI, he was still feeling his way, and this would be his first agency review. At the meeting the book-club division would be represented by Joe Blackwell and me from editorial; Leroy and his boss, Jim Hacker, the group marketing director; and Janie Mengers, who is in charge of the monthly MSI club bulletins, the brochures that tell members what books have been chosen. The theory is that there should be some sort of coordination between the advertising campaigns that bring in the members and the selling material that is sent to them afterward. It is a theory that has never gotten off the ground, partly because the marketing directors keep changing and so do the advertising campaigns. But the members go right on buying the books—in gratifying numbers—from Janie's neatly stylized bulletins. She is very good at her job and we work together quite amicably.

The agency on MSI for the past seven months has been Lothrop and Logan, and they would be sending along an account executive, an art director, and a copywriter, together with a battery of charts, graphs, past ads, and future possibilities.

The Lothrop and Logan people were already in the conference room when we straggled in, the editors prompt, as always, the business side late, as usual. The account executive was supervising the art director, who was setting up easels for the charts and graphs. There was also a slide projector and a screen, so it looked as if we'd be in for a really long, boring session.

At the last minute Nate Meyer came in, too. All marketing directors are invited to all agency reviews, on the theory that they might learn something they could incorporate in campaigns for the other clubs. My theory is that they don't have much else to do, but perhaps it's just that Nate rubs me the wrong way.

Leroy made all the necessary introductions and then turned to Art Logan, the account executive. (Art happens to be a nephew of the Logan who founded the agency, but I haven't figured out if that relationship is a plus or minus.)

Art began with a review of the past three years and managed to deprecate every ad created before Lothrop and Logan got its hands on the account. Nate fidgeted through part of that; even though he had brought Lothrop and Logan in himself, he had had a hand in the ads immediately preceding the current campaign, and adverse comments were a reflection on him, he thought.

I used to get mad in these review sessions, too, but for a different reason. According to the agency, any agency, when an ad worked, it was because it was brilliant. When it didn't, it was because the book list was lousy. They could never see it the other way around: that good books make the ad effective, but a lousy presentation could ruin the whole thing. Marcia had pulled me aside before my very first agency review and explained that this was a mind-set of all account executives, and I shouldn't worry about it. Approached from a different angle, account executives could be handled. She was right, as usual.

Nate and Art and the copywriter got into a wrangle about something or other, all past history, and Leroy was too inexperienced to handle it. Luckily, Jim Hacker, the group marketing director, put in a calming word, and we got back on the track. Nate was still muttering under his breath, though, and he turned to Joe and said something about the sensitivity of all copywriters, and did Joe remember what had happened in the RC agency review two weeks before. Joe merely looked uncomfortable, and I wondered what Nate was running on about.

At noon we were still arguing about last year's campaign, and Jim Hacker made the decision that we'd better send out for sandwiches and work straight through the lunch hour. Joe groaned, but we had both expected it. These things always drag out to interminable lengths. Jim called in his secretary, who took the sandwich orders, and then everybody got up and stretched, and I dashed back to my office to see if anything interesting had happened.

Abby told me that Lieutenant Jack Morrison had stopped by, on his way to see the president, George Griffith. Jack had seemed disappointed that I wasn't there (good), but all he had wanted to do was drop off my raincoat, which I had left in his car (oh). Abby had asked him about the case, but he said nothing much had happened at the funeral, which was what I had said, too. Then she asked him about whether she should phone Ricardo again, and he had been surprised. But when she said that she thought it might be a good idea to call him because maybe he could tell her where Shirley was, he said to go ahead. Abby thought it was funny that Jack hadn't thought of calling Ricardo himself, but I didn't enlighten her. Anyway, she made the phone call while Jack was standing right there, and Ricardo had let loose a stream of Spanish, cursing her, she thought. He didn't know where Shirley was, he kept insisting, but Abby wondered if he was telling the truth.

"He called me *despalomada,*" Abby said. "Imagine that. Jack said it meant pigeon-brained, and he said it's his favorite word for the people he has met on this case; but I think he was joking."

I hoped so. It might apply to Elly, in a way, but I hoped he wasn't extending it beyond that—to Abby, say, or to Meredith, or to me.

There were no other messages of interest, so I reluctantly drifted back to the conference room.

We were still in the middle of the break, waiting for delivery of the lunch order. Joe was looking unhappy, trapped by Nate Meyer and Jim Hacker, so I wandered over to see what the problem was. Nate was still fussing about copywriters, and he referred again to the Readers' Circle agency review two weeks before.

I turned to Joe to find out what that was all about, while Nate and Jim Hacker went off on a tangent of their own about the legal wording in the coupons. Such minute hairs to split. If the Federal Trade Commission says we have to say it that way, we should do it and not quibble so much.

Anyway, Joe was trying to remember what had triggered Nate's anger at the RC meeting. "We were just having our usual arguments," Joe said. "You know how it is, Karen. Marcia was always pressing to make sure that the newest and strongest books were in the ads, and Nate was getting defensive because somebody had screwed up and three current best-sellers had been left out of the last *Times* ad. And then he got into a fight with the copywriter, Dick Frazier, who is always trying to get more sex into the ads. Dick has this theory that all you need to make a novel into a best-seller is a couple of really raunchy scenes, and he thinks we should try some kind of approach like that in our ads."

"How would he do that?"

"He'd like to feature one sexy book in the ad and pull out a couple of paragraphs from the steamiest scene—whet the reader's interest, make him join the club to find out what happened."

"And Nate didn't like the idea?"

"Sometimes you can't tell with him. Maybe he was just mad because he hadn't thought it up himself."

"What did Marcia say?"

"She just sat back listening. She knew it would never get off the ground, so there was no point wasting her breath on it. I took my cue from her. And sure enough, the whole thing kind of sputtered out. Except Nate said that Dick could fiddle around with some copy for a test ad in *Cosmopolitan* if he wanted to. I don't think that Marcia heard that, though, because she was talking to George about something else at that point."

"Well, it's your headache now, Joe."

"Yes, but who knows for how long?"

And then the sandwiches came, and Leroy spilled his coffee, and it was after one o'clock before we got back to the slides.

George Griffith came in at 2:30, while we were discussing possible ads for the fall campaign. I was in the middle of explaining why I liked the straight copy approach better than the ads featuring a trembling, threatened girl, and I think Leroy was ready to agree with me until Jim Hacker butted in on the other side. So of course Leroy sided with his boss. I looked to Joe for a little support, but it was George who cut in first, to agree with me. That shut up Jim and effectively ended the meeting, too. Whatever George wanted, he got. That's the nice thing about being president. How lucky in this case that it worked out for the best—*my* way.

I collected my papers and exchanged knowing glances with Janie Mengers. Janie always keeps her mouth shut at these reviews, trying not to call attention to herself. She once told me that she was glad everybody argued about ads and never touched on her domain; that way she could keep it all to herself. So, from her point of view, she had won again.

Jim Hacker had lingered to talk to George. He was always making excuses to do that, buttering him up with the most outrageous flattery. I hope I never want to be a vice president that much.

Joe had already slipped out, and I was ready to follow him when George called me over, cutting off Jim in mid-sentence.

"We'll talk about it later," George was saying, a hint of impatience creeping into his voice. Jim nodded hastily and made a big show of supervising Leroy's good-bys to the account executive.

"Come to my office, Karen," George said, and his voice was brusque. I was immediately intimidated.

I followed him to his corner aerie with the sweeping view of the Hudson and all of lower Manhattan. On clear days—and this was a rare one—you could see all the way to the Statue of Liberty and the Verrazano Bridge. I wondered how George could ever get any work done, but perhaps he had stopped seeing it by now. Jaded. Blasé. He might as well pull the drapes and forget about it.

"I suppose you're wondering why I called you in, Karen," George said, closing the door.

I jerked my attention away from the great outdoors and watched him taking his place behind the massive rosewood desk. He motioned me to one of the leather chairs facing him and I sat down, reminding myself that I was not a servant and I didn't know how to tug at my forelock without messing up my hair. So I put on a tentative smile and waited.

George seemed to be having trouble getting started himself, and maybe that was a good sign. Or maybe not. It was always painfully awkward to fire anybody. I raked over the recent past and wondered what I had done wrong. The Agatha Christie project? We had had a lot of talk about offering a forty-volume set of her mysteries in matched bindings, but Leroy was supposed to do a cost analysis before I started clearing book-club rights.

"You were admiring the view," George began.

"Yes, it's great today, isn't it?" This is pretty inane, I was thinking, but it occurred to me that George was just as uncomfortable as I was, and that immediately calmed me down. Now that I looked at him again, he seemed downright jumpy, and those beautifully manicured hands —why, he was making a real effort to keep them steady while he lighted a cigarette.

"Lieutenant Morrison admired the view, too," George said, and I swallowed a smile. George is about as subtle as a Mack truck.

"Yes. Lieutenant Morrison would appreciate an opportunity to see New York from this angle," I said.

"He came to see me this morning."

I nodded encouragingly. Was *I* putting *him* at his ease?

"He said you had given him a lot of information about how the book-club division operates."

"I was trying to cooperate," I said. But I didn't like this turn in the conversation at all.

"Yes, of course, we must all cooperate, Karen." A little authority was creeping back into his voice, and I sat up straighter.

"But, Karen, there is no need for you to speculate with him about who will be the next editorial director of the RC book clubs. Or the next managing editor, either."

"I'm sorry. He was asking questions, you see, looking for motives. I mean, he's trying to find out who killed Marcia, after all."

"I'm perfectly aware of that, Karen. But it's absurd to think that anyone on the staff is guilty."

"Yes, I told him that, too."

"And it's absurd to think that anything I might have said three weeks ago would have caused anyone to kill Marcia."

So that was it. Bull's-eye. Jack had been trying out his theory of the mythical editor John Terrific, and he had scored a solid hit.

"It certainly seems unlikely," I said.

"Unlikely? It's impossible! I was having lunch with Barry Tremont, and our conversation was strictly confidential."

Barry is president and publisher of Berwyn Paperbacks, on exactly the same corporate level as George, who is president of Berwyn Book Clubs. So John Terrific must be one of Barry's paperback editors. I bet it's Stan Ryden, the executive editor. He's the one who scored a real coup, buying the witchcraft novel that's the biggest thing since *The Exorcist*.

I smothered a triumphant grin, and George just looked at me, a little puzzled.

"I'm sure you explained it all satisfactorily," I said.

"Naturally. But he is a peculiar man, Lieutenant Morrison."

I looked at George expectantly.

"He reminds me of a college professor I knew at the B School," he went on reminiscently. "Gridley had a way of guiding you through a conversation and wringing the last drop of information out of you. Once when I was working on a case study . . ." His voice trailed off as he looked at me and remembered where he was. And who he was, too.

"Karen, I called you in here to remind you to be careful in your dealings with the police. Now, I understand from Lieutenant Morrison that he spent a good deal of time with you Saturday."

"He just happened to drive me home from Marcia's funeral," I said. Like I just happened to be sitting in that coffee shop when Ricardo was arrested.

"Yes. Did it ever occur to you that he might have arranged that deliberately?"

"Well, yes, it did cross my mind."

"He's devious, Karen. He may even suspect *you*. You know that you can demand to have a lawyer present when he questions you."

"George! What are you saying? I don't have anything to hide."

"Of course not," he agreed hastily. "It's just that this policeman

84

might twist what you're saying, and it could become very awkward for you. And for the Berwyn Publishing Company, too."

It occurred to me, not for the first time, that I don't like George T. Griffith at all. Not at all.

"I'll certainly be careful, George," I said. I wondered suddenly if *he* had anything to hide, but that was absurd, too. I'd be suspecting my own mother if Jack didn't solve this case pretty soon.

There seemed to be no point in hanging around, but George was unwilling to let me leave on a sour note, so he gave me a little soft soap about how right I had been in the agency meeting, and then we both agreed that MSI was flourishing mightily. And that was that.

I could hardly wait to tell Jack.

He wasn't there when I telephoned him, and a woman's voice took the message.

"Tell him Miss Lindstrom called. Karen Lindstrom."

"Carolyn Lindstrom?"

"No. Karen. K A R E N."

"All right. I have that. And what is the message, Miss Lindstrom?"

"Just ask him to call me. It's important."

"Yes, I'll do that. Thank you."

"Thank you."

Now, who could *she* be? It was an older voice, an educated voice, but definitely New York. I brooded about it all the while I read through my In Box and tossed the contents into my wastebasket.

At five o'clock Jerry stopped by my office and suggested we go out for a drink, and Lucy and Beth (she's the editor of the Movie Story Book Club) joined us. I don't think I was very good company, and the only interesting thing that happened was that I ran into Terry Kerman as we were leaving. Terry was having a drink with a man I didn't recognize, and she didn't bother to introduce him.

We exchanged greetings and she said she'd call me for lunch, which I thought was highly unlikely. On the other hand, maybe she didn't know that I knew about her and Joe Blackwell. Surely the police had been around to see her by now, but maybe Jack had avoided mentioning my name. I certainly hoped so.

Jack was waiting for me when I got home, sitting in his car, parked in the no-parking zone.

"I just happened to be passing through the neighborhood," he said, "and I thought I'd stop by."

I laughed, and he got out of the car and followed me inside. "Actually, I've been waiting ten minutes, and it occurred to me that you might be staked out waiting for *me* somewhere. But then I realized I wasn't arresting anybody, so you had to be on your way home. Where were you?"

"You always want to know everything."

"Sure. Where were you?"

"Having a drink with three other editors." I picked up my mail and we went upstairs together, just as if I had invited him in.

"I got your message," he said, settling down at my desk as if he belonged there. And out came the inevitable notebook.

"My message. Yes. Who was it who answered your phone?"

"My mother."

"Your *mother?*"

"Yes, really and truly. My mother. What did you think?"

"I don't know. Your mother?"

"Well, she has a key to my apartment," he said defensively. "Actually, she and Dad live in Bayside, but when I was just out of the hospital a year ago I gave them a key, and she used to come over for a few hours during the day and sort of look after me."

"I see. What were you doing in the hospital?"

"*You* always want to know everything."

"Sure. What were you doing in the hospital?"

"Do you ever get the feeling there's an echo around here?"

"Frequently. What were you doing in the hospital?"

"I was recovering from a gunshot wound. In my chest. It was a little messy at the time, but I'm perfectly all right now."

"I see. It sure beats those rice paddies in Vietnam, doesn't it?"

"But the natives speak my language."

"OK. Why was your mother in your apartment today?"

"She was bringing me some homemade peach ice cream, if you really have to know. Putting it in my refrigerator. They had made a freezerful yesterday, and had half expected me to drop by; and when I didn't, Mother came by my apartment today on her way to her cousin's in Woodside. She phoned first. All right? Got that?"

"I'm making mental notes," I said.

"For your information, I am not an only child. But my sister lives in San Diego with her husband and three children, and that's too far to send ice cream."

"OK. OK. I like peach ice cream, too."

"Good. What did you want to tell me?"

"Well." I stretched out on the couch as if I were at a psychoanalyst's and prepared to do full justice to my conversation with George T. Griffith. Jack is really a very good listener.

"And then he said he had lunch with Barry Tremont," I rambled on, well into my monologue. "Barry is publisher of Berwyn Paperbacks."

"Yes, I got that out of George Griffith, too, before he clammed up on me. I went around to see this Barry Tremont afterward, but he was taking a long weekend in Easthampton and won't be back until tomorrow. George wouldn't tell me what names came up at lunch three weeks ago, but I think I can probably get the information out of Tremont."

"But I've already guessed who it is, your mysterious editor John Terrific."

"Yes?"

I explained about Stan Ryden and his coup with the witchcraft book.

"You're probably right," Jack agreed. "I'll get Tremont to confirm it tomorrow. Unless George Griffith gets to him first and turns him off."

"I don't think that will happen. I don't think Barry Tremont would take George Griffith's advice on anything."

"So. Like that, is it?"

"Yes. The next big prize is executive vice president of the whole Berwyn Publishing Company, and they're both jockeying for position."

I stood up and stretched, and it occurred to me that I ought to offer Jack a drink or something. He declined, but suggested dinner around the corner on 86th Street. I had had only half a sandwich at that miserable agency lunch and was starved, so I accepted with alacrity. One of these days, probably, I'd have to invite Jack to dinner, but I hate cooking and I always have trouble making everything come out done at the same time. Some of the rites of courtship are a pain in the neck.

Eighty-sixth Street is lined with restaurants of every nationality, and we chose Spanish that night, mostly because I knew a place that served terrific *sangría,* and I was thirsty. Jack ordered a whole pitcher, and we had each drained a glass by the time we decided on the paella.

"I've never had the paella here," I said, "so I can't vouch for it."

"Well, I have, and I do." Jack signaled the waiter, who had suddenly found room on his face for a smile. The service had improved in this place since my last visit.

"You know your way around the New York restaurant scene, don't you?" I said, after he had ordered dinner for both of us.

"I've eaten my way across Eighty-sixth Street."

"That sounds like a good project."

"It was my wife's idea. She didn't much like to cook."

"Neither do I."

"That makes it unanimous, doesn't it?"

I pondered that and decided, on the whole, it was better to get back to the murder case.

"Did you call Mrs. Dimaria today, Jack?"

"I didn't, but Janet reached her. Janet is a detective," he explained, to forestall my obvious question. "We decided it would be less threatening if a woman called. Actually, I think Janet concocted some story about a telephone survey for a new toothpaste. It seemed a little far-fetched to me, but she had a point."

"What point?"

"Well, you don't exactly call a woman out of the blue and ask her who her niece's dentist is. She'll ask why you want to know, and if you tell her you want to identify a body, you'll upset her, probably without cause. I think it's a very long shot that it's Shirley Hastings in the morgue."

"I see. So this Janet calls and asks a few questions about toothpaste and then works the conversation around to dentists and finds out that way."

"Right. It worked like a charm, but Janet didn't reach Mrs. Dimaria until almost five, just before I phoned in. That's when I found out you had called, by the way. My mother had phoned in your message. I should have given you that number, too. Let me write it down for you."

He tore a page out of his notebook and jotted down his name and district-unit phone number. I looked at it, memorized it, and dropped the paper in my handbag.

"So you don't know if Janet reached Shirley's dentist yet?"

"It turned out that she had two, one of them an orthodontist. No, Janet hadn't had a chance to call either of them yet. This isn't the only case we're working on, you know."

"But this is the most interesting," I hazarded.

"By far," he agreed.

I waited for him to expand on that, but he didn't, and we were distracted by the arrival of the paella. He was right: it was very good.

I was discarding the last of the clam shells when I remembered about Ted Ferris, Marcia's lawyer. Jack had expected to see him today.

He acknowledged paying him a visit, but the only thing he volunteered willingly was that Ferris had had a bandage on his right forearm. Jack waited for my reaction and got it.

"It was a bullet wound? You mean that theory I had about Marcia firing the gun at her murderer was right?"

"No. But I must admit I was shaken when I walked into Ferris's office and saw part of a bandage protruding from his jacket sleeve. I couldn't believe that we were solving the case because of one blithe remark from you."

"I can't believe it either."

"Well, relax; it didn't happen that way. It wasn't a bullet wound at all. He was up on the Cape and he accidentally put his fist through a window and cut his arm on the glass shards."

"Accidentally put his fist through a window?"

"Hard to believe, isn't it? I think he was drunk and he was taking a swing at somebody who ducked. He was reluctant to talk about it, as you can imagine."

"Are you just going to take his word that that's the way it happened?"

"Karen, you know me better than that."

"You're checking it out and following up some leads."

"Right."

"And you found out the name of his girl friend."

"Yes."

"And she was with him at the Cape."

"Yes. Are we playing Twenty Questions?"

"Don't distract me. Have you talked to her yet?"

"Yes."

"Well, what happened? Tell me."

"She was reluctant to talk about it, too. Particularly on the phone."

"But you have seen her?"

"Not yet. I have an appointment with her—" he consulted his watch—"fifty minutes from now."

I looked at my watch, too. It was 8:10. "That's a funny time to make an appointment."

He shrugged. "I didn't argue about it. Anyway, it gave me a chance to have dinner with you."

I paused over that remark, and it was tempting, but I pushed on. "Does she live around here?"

"Yes. But if you think I'm going to give you her name and address, you're crazy. Anyway, you don't know her."

"She's not in publishing?"

"No. Let's talk about something else. Aren't you interested that I read Marcia's book yesterday?"

"Mildly. Did you find out anything?"

"Not much. I'm sure it's at least partly autobiographical, but it ends with the girl at age nineteen and her brother twenty-one. The father disappears halfway through, and he's altogether a very shadowy figure. The character of the mother emerges very strongly, though; it's the best-realized part of the book."

"You're turning into quite a critic. Maybe you could do some part-time reading for the clubs."

"I'd be about as effective there as you would be on the police force."

"That's a two-edged remark."

"It was meant to be."

"All right, all right. Anything else about the book?"

"No. It was very mild, very clean. I can see why it didn't become an enormous success. What I can't see is why the murderer walked off with it."

I thought about that. "Maybe it wasn't the book itself. I mean, maybe it wasn't the contents of the novel. Maybe it was something about that specific copy of the book."

"You mean an inscription in it or something?"

"I guess so. I don't know what I mean. A secret cipher . . . Something out of a Hitchcock movie. You know, pin pricks under certain letters in the third chapter. You spell it out and it proves the Nazis will bomb Pearl Harbor."

"That was the Japanese."

"I know that, for heaven's sake. I'm just inventing a new plot for you."

"Thanks, but I have enough on my plate already. And that reminds me . . ." He caught the waiter's attention and ordered coffee. For once we were both ready to skip dessert.

"What's going on in your world, Karen? Any of your friends behaving suspiciously?"

"No. That is, Meredith phoned me today while I was in the agency review meeting, but I didn't call back. Abby said she was just calling to make sure I was all right. Do you know she called me five times Saturday night to check up on me? She thought maybe you had arrested me. Or something."

"She's an excitable lady."

"I guess so. And I ran into Terry Kerman after work today. She was having drinks with some man I didn't know. She didn't introduce him, either."

"That must have really bothered you."

I shot him a dirty look, but we both laughed. "She said she'd call me for lunch, but I doubt if she will. Did you mention my name to her when you were checking up on Joe?"

91

"No. Karen, if she doesn't call you in the next day or two, why don't you phone her?"

"You mean you want me to have lunch with her?"

"Yes. It's nothing vital, of course, but I think she may have been holding something back."

"Like what?"

"I don't know. Don't bother if you don't want to. It was just a passing thought."

I sighed heavily and pulled a scrap of paper out of my handbag. It was the same paper he had given me with his phone number. "Call Terry," I printed in black ink.

I looked at him speculatively, but he changed the subject.

"What was this agency review that you were in today?"

I went off into a long, detailed explanation of that, which led me to explain about marketing directors, and the brush warfare between them and editors.

"But what do they do that's so bad?" Jack asked.

"You really want to know?" He nodded, and I plunged ahead. "Well, for instance, when I took over MSI I inherited a real kook. Matthew Davis, his name was."

"That doesn't sound so kooky."

"No? Well, Matt's parents had been missionaries in South America, and I think he grew up with some remote Indian tribe. At any rate, he didn't mingle with the rest of the world until he came to the States to go to college. And then I guess he went wild. Got involved with two girls at once; they were *both* pregnant, I think. I was never very clear on that story. But he had a brilliant scholastic record at Williams, in spite of everything; it's just that he didn't have any common sense at all."

"How did that affect you?"

"Well, Matt was marketing director for both MSI and the Sports Book Club, and the same ad agency was working on both accounts. He had some crazy idea about combining the two clubs. And when he saw he couldn't get anywhere with that, he decided he could prove his point by advertising MSI in sports publications on a test basis. You see, Berwyn has this group of specialized magazines, and the clubs can advertise in them at house rates. It's a complicated accounting procedure, but essentially it's money out of one corporate pocket and into another. The ads are charged to the book clubs and have to be justified in some kind of cost-accounting analysis, but I don't understand all that. The point is that Matt put MSI ads into the tennis, football, and baseball magazines. He had this crazy idea that tennis players could read mysteries while they were waiting for a court, or baseball fans could use the seventh-inning stretch to pop another chapter of Agatha Christie."

"That's wild."

"Yes. Eventually, Jerry and I put the skids under him, but it took some doing. The man who was group marketing director at the time had hired Matt in the first place, and he didn't want to hear about anything going wrong."

"So what did you do?"

"We explained it all to Marcia, and she somehow clued in George Griffith. For once George moved promptly, and Matt was eased out. And then the group marketing director disappeared back into the woodwork at Phoenix Industries, from whence he came. The last I heard about Matt, he was selling beauty kits in a franchise operation and positively thriving."

"So he would have nothing against Marcia."

"No. He never knew what hit him. After Matt we had Anya Rosoff, but she went to work for the CIA."

"You're making this up."

"Have I ever lied to you?" I elaborated on Anya's supposed relationship to the last czar, and we speculated on her value to the government deciphering the true annual production rate of Russian widgets. Reluctantly, Jack discarded the idea that she could have had anything at all to do with the murder.

That brought us to Nate Meyer, who succeeded her as marketing director of MSI before he was promoted to the Readers' Circle job.

"What's so obnoxious about him?"

"It's his whole superior attitude. He's always convinced he's right, and he barely listens to anybody else, though of course he has to follow orders from Jim Hacker, the group marketing director."

"Did Nate clash with Marcia?"

"He clashed with everybody. But you see, Marcia didn't exactly clash. She didn't see any point in fighting just for the sake of a fight, and Nate likes nothing better. There was an agency review for RC just two weeks ago, but the big fight there was between Nate and the copywriter. Joe was there, but he said Marcia didn't get involved. It was something about making the ads sexier, quoting scenes from a book."

"How was it resolved?"

"I don't think it was, exactly. There was some talk about preparing a test ad, but Joe didn't think anybody would follow through on it."

"That sounds rather slipshod."

"Yes, that's fairly typical."

Jack thought about that a minute and then jotted down something in his notebook. He was going to get in touch with Nate Meyer, I was sure. And that would certainly be an interesting confrontation.

I reached for the coffee pot, but we had emptied it. The waiter hurried over to bring us more, but Jack glanced at his watch and shot out of his seat. "I'm late. Let's get out of here." He pressed some bills on the waiter and didn't wait for change.

We covered the three blocks back to my apartment in record time, and Jack dashed for his car as soon as I had my front door unlocked. He called out a good night, but any answer I might have made was lost in the slam of his car door and the sudden leap of the engine. So it was ten minutes after nine; the coach wasn't going to turn into a pumpkin, and there would always be space in a no-parking zone in some other neighborhood. He had headed south on York Avenue, but that was no clue at all. Oh, well. I couldn't believe that Ted Ferris's current girl friend was going to be of much use in solving this case.

++++++

6

++++++

Terry Kerman surprised me the next morning by phoning and suggesting we have lunch that very day. I was supposed to be seeing an editor from Atheneum, but he would be understanding about postponing our date, so Terry and I settled on 12:30 at the St. Regis.

Much to my surprise, she was already there when I arrived, and I was a minute early myself. Whatever it was, she was eager to see me. I hadn't talked to her for more than five minutes in the last two years.

We ordered spritzers (it occurred to me that Joe Blackwell always orders spritzers, too), and I smiled brightly, waiting for her to begin.

Terry is considerably more subtle than George Griffith, though, and we had reached dessert before she got around to Marcia's murder. In the meantime, we had had a pleasant jaunt through the old days at Doubleday, when we had both been in the publicity department; and then I learned considerably more about the inner workings of picture research at Time-Life than I really wanted to know.

That's how we got to the murder. Somehow Terry had got her hands on the press pictures from last Tuesday, when Marcia's body had been carried out of her building on West End Avenue. The magazines hadn't used them, though. The murder had not made either *Time* or *Newsweek;* I had zipped through the office copies that morning, looking.

I told Terry that the detectives had been around to see all of us last Tuesday, and they had been checking records and following through on leads.

Terry can recognize a cliché as well as anybody else, and I realized I wasn't being fair. She was taking me out to lunch to find out

95

something, and I was there for the same reason. We weren't going to get anywhere being too cautious.

So I told her that I had seen Lieutenant Morrison several times, and he seemed to be talking to practically everybody in publishing, everybody with even a remote connection to Marcia.

So Terry said he had been to see her, too, and I kept my face blank and asked why.

She poured herself another cup of coffee, but I knew that if she had come this far, she wasn't going to stall and turn back now. And she didn't.

"Karen, if I tell you something, will you promise not to tell anybody else?"

"Well, yes, Terry. But if it's about the murder, I don't see how I can keep anything from Jack. From Lieutenant Morrison," I amended hastily.

She looked at me curiously for a minute, but let it pass. "He's all right. That is, he knows anyway. Just don't tell anyone else."

"OK, I won't. I promise."

"Well, then, Karen, I happened to be with Joe Blackwell last Monday."

"Oh?"

"Yes, we met for dinner. And then we had kind of an argument. I was trying to break off with him, if you really want to know the truth. I've met somebody else—you saw him last night, as a matter of fact."

I waited expectantly, but she didn't identify him by name or occupation, and I didn't press.

"The thing is," Terry went on, "I don't want him to know about Joe. That's over. I was crazy to get involved with Joe in the first place. He's nice enough and all that, but . . . Is he going to take over Marcia's job, Karen?"

"I hope so. But it hasn't been decided yet."

"Do the police really suspect him? That is, do you think he'll be tried? Because if he is, I'll be subpoenaed to give testimony, and that will really wreck things."

So that's what was eating her. But why was she telling *me?*

She explained, and I didn't much like her chain of thought. "Karen,

I haven't seen Joe since last Monday, but we've talked on the phone a lot. He had to tell me that he gave my name to Lieutenant Morrison. Joe tried to keep me out of this, partly because of Dotty, but this detective was really hounding him."

"Yes, I guess he was."

"Joe says he's been seeing a lot of you, too."

"He happened to drive me home from the funeral Saturday."

"I know. Joe said Meredith Baker talked of nothing else all the way back from Philadelphia. She couldn't make up her mind whether he was arresting you or attacking you."

"She gets a little carried away."

"I don't know her. But Joe said that Lieutenant Morrison couldn't possibly suspect you. He just has a gleam in his eye where you're concerned, Joe said, and the two of you are . . . getting to be close friends."

"He's trying to solve the murder," I protested, "and he's interested in the whole publishing scene." It didn't sound very convincing to me, either.

"So I thought you'd probably know," Terry went on.

"Know what?"

"Why, know what he's thinking, who he's going to arrest. If it's not Joe, I won't have to be a witness, don't you see?"

I saw. I also saw that with Meredith and Joe and Terry all talking at once, it was going to be all over publishing that I was having an affair with Lieutenant Jack Morrison, and everyone would know except Jack and me.

I assured Terry that it was most unlikely that she would have to testify to her whereabouts last Monday. And I made a mental note to tell Jack that the only thing she was hiding was the presence of a new man in her life. And she hadn't even told me his name. Some detective I was turning out to be.

Terry signed for the lunch, and she left the restaurant considerably more light-hearted than I was.

Nate Meyer charged into my office that afternoon, and I could have predicted the first words out of his mouth: "Lieutenant Morrison was here to see me."

97

He was raging, spoiling for a fight, and I needed a little emotional release, too.

"Karen, what the hell are you doing? Why are you sicking your boy friend on me?"

"He is *not* my boy friend. I didn't sick him on you. And if you don't have anything to hide, what the hell is the matter with *you?*"

"Damned nosy cop. It's no goddamned business of his where I was last Monday or any other Monday."

"He's investigating a murder. What's the matter? Are you afraid he'll find out something?"

"I do not go around killing people. Though, by God, if I had a gun right now I might start with you."

Abby appeared in the doorway, looking a little anxious. "We can hear you all over the floor."

"Good," I said. "Maybe I'll need a few witnesses for these threats."

"*You* are a first-class idiot," Nate said.

"Oh, shut up. If you're going to indulge in childish insults, you can get out right now. If you have anything interesting to say, I'll give you five minutes."

Abby hovered uncertainly in the doorway, but she retreated hastily when Nate took a step in her direction.

"Do you want me to do anything, Karen?" she asked.

"No, I guess not. You might as well close the door, and I'll give this wild man a chance to calm down and turn rational, if he can."

Nate glared at her, but he stopped pacing and sat down across from me and pulled a cigarette out of his pocket. Out of habit, he offered me one, and then he laughed at the ridiculousness of the situation.

"Really, Karen, I'm damned mad you dragged me into this."

"Oh, use your head, Nate. The police were bound to get around to you, to everybody who knew Marcia, sooner or later. They've been through the editorial department with a fine-tooth comb. Why should *you* escape?"

"Stupid idiot! Do you know what he was after?"

"Tell me."

"He wanted to know what Marcia thought of the fall advertising campaign for Readers' Circle. Can you imagine! He wanted to know if she was throwing roadblocks in my way, making me change anything. How could she make me change anything? I'm the one running the advertising side of this outfit."

"Modest, self-effacing Nate."

"Rubbish. And who are you to sit in judgment? You weren't there. Morrison wanted to know if there were any fights. Hell, of course there were fights. Those agency guys are a pain in the ass. Particularly the copywriter, Dick Frazier. Shooting off his mouth in front of George and everybody. Maybe it's time to switch agencies again."

"I thought Jim Hacker just assigned the RC account a year ago to Coleman, Kressman, or whatever it is."

"Coleman, Kressman, and Yates. He did. But he's not the marketing director of RC any more. *I* am."

"But he's your boss. Anyway, I don't see how you can go around switching agencies all the time. They can never get a handle on what they're doing."

"A lot you know about it. Why don't editors just stick to their books and leave the important decisions to us?"

"*You* are the most conceited, arrogant idiot on the whole Berwyn staff. Even with all the competition."

"*You* talk about arrogance! God, you're all impossible. Even Marcia, sitting there quietly, ready to spring her little traps. Leading George Griffith around like a poodle on a leash."

Nate ground out his cigarette and stalked to the door. "But I did not kill her. And you can just call off your precious Lieutenant Morrison and tell him to go to hell."

"Why don't you tell him yourself?"

"I did. He said he's considered it, but on the whole he preferred New York."

I laughed, and then Nate did, too.

"All the same, Karen, I wouldn't trust him an inch. Are you really serious about him?"

"What's got into you? What's got into everybody? Nothing is going on between me and Lieutenant Morrison, and it wouldn't be anybody's business anyway."

"You're too damned touchy. You'll probably even make a big thing out of the fact I yelled at you. I yell at everybody. That way I don't get ulcers."

"No, you give them." But I guess he was sort of apologizing.

"All right, I'll even let you have the last word. What will it be?"

"Good-by."

He gave a half salute and departed, and both Abby and Jerry popped in to see if he had left any scars.

"No. He's full of sound and fury, signifying nothing."

Abby looked relieved, and then she told me that Leroy Langner had stopped by to see me, and would I please go around to his office.

So I did. Leroy just wanted to talk about MSI ads. He had the roughs that the agency had left yesterday, and we quickly agreed on which ones we liked best. From his obvious sigh of relief, I could tell that Jim Hacker had chosen the same ones I did. It looked as if things would be going swimmingly in MSI for a change. Leroy was so grateful that he invited me to lunch next day.

I had to pass George Griffith's office on my way back, and I did a double-take when I saw Stan Ryden standing in the doorway, on his way either in or out. I stopped at the water cooler to see which it was, to be ready with a greeting if he headed my way, toward the elevators and his office two floors up.

As executive editor of Berwyn Paperbacks, Stan Ryden rarely put in an appearance on the book-club floor. There were two possible reasons for his presence today in George's office, and I didn't like either of them: either Geroge was sizing him up for Marcia's job, or the two of them were discussing the murder investigation.

Stan was so bemused by whatever it was that I almost had to trip him to make him notice me. He came out of his daze, full of apologies, and full of the kind of charm he can turn on at will. I was on guard immediately.

"Karen, I'm so glad I ran into you. And almost literally, at that." Stan has a kind of lopsided smile, and I suppose some girl once told him it was devastating. I suspect a partial muscle paralysis, myself, but it does give him a disarming little-boy look, and he plays it for all he's worth.

"Stan! What brings you down among us?" Why should I beat around the bush?

"Ah." He lowered his voice conspiratorially. "We were just talking about you, and the murder case, and the memorial service."

"Really? Tell me about it."

He looked around doubtfully to see if we were being overheard, so I led him back to my office. I wasn't eager to have George come out and see us together.

Abby looked up in some surprise, and with some distaste, too. I think Stan had once made a pass at her at an office Christmas party. But it wasn't the pass that bothered her so much; it was the fact that he had forgotten all about it next day. He didn't seem to recognize her now, either.

"Well, Karen," he said, settling into my visitor's chair. "Lieutenant Morrison came by to see us."

I wished I had a dollar for every time somebody told me that. But at least Stan sounded pleased, not angry.

"You know," he went on, "I've always found police work fascinating. When I was a kid, I even played around with the idea of becoming a private eye." The boyish smile appeared again, and I realized that Jack had conned Stan into playing detective with him.

"Do tell me what happened." I refrained from batting my eyes, but it's almost impossible to overplay a scene with Stan. He's acting all the time, walking around as if a spotlight is following him constantly. That curly hair, the dark flashing eyes, the perpetually tanned face, the lopsided grin— he belongs in Hollywood. Actor John Terrific as well as Editor John Terrific. Murderer John Terrific, too? Never. It spoils the image.

"I'm not quite sure what it was all about, actually," Stan said, leaning forward conspiratorially. "You see, Lieutenant Morrison was talking to Barry Tremont first. You know Barry—he's publisher of Berwyn Paperbacks."

I nodded impatiently. Stan always explains the obvious.

"Well, Barry called me in and introduced Lieutenant Morrison. And then Barry asked me if I remembered that George Griffith had complimented me on buying the witchcraft book. And of course I did." Stan was preening himself almost visibly.

"I understand it's an enormous success, Stan."

"Yes, we've just ordered another six-hundred-thousand printing."

"And that's all Barry said? Did you remember that George had complimented you?"

"Yes. Strange, wasn't it? I mean, it's not as if George had been the only one who complimented me on that."

"No, I guess not." I suppressed a grin. "And you hadn't heard that George said anything else? That he might be interested in having you at the book clubs, for instance?"

"No. Isn't it funny that you should say that? Lieutenant Morrison asked the very same thing."

Well, I guess that proved something. That Barry Tremont was discreet and didn't go around repeating his luncheon conversations with George Griffith. And thus Stan would not have had any motive to go kill Marcia. And so another of Jack's theories bit the dust.

"I'll tell you what *my* theory is, Karen," Stan confided.

"Oh, yes, do." This time I *did* bat my eyes. What the hell.

Stan didn't even notice—he was too absorbed in playing Junior G-Man. "Karen, I think she committed suicide. I really do. I know it's a terrible thing to say about anyone, but she seemed awfully depressed the last time I saw her."

"When was that?"

"Three or four weeks ago. She was having a drink at the Algonquin with some man I didn't know, and she didn't see me. And she just looked awful. I don't know what he was saying to her, but she was looking miserable. I told Lieutenant Morrison."

"What did he say?"

"He seemed interested and asked me to describe the man."

"I see." I supposed that had been Ted Ferris with her, breaking off their affair.

"And the other reason I don't think she was murdered," Stan went on, "is that she didn't have any enemies. Everybody liked her, Karen. You know that."

I agreed, and it seemed to me that we were right back to Square One. Except how could it be suicide when she was shot twice?

I had no answer for anything.

"You'll be at the memorial service on Thursday, won't you, Karen?" Stan asked.

I nodded.

"Then I'll see you there," Stan said. "George asked me to deliver a brief tribute. That's why I was in his office, reading him my speech."

"Oh, I see."

"Yes. He wanted a representative from Berwyn, outside the clubs, and he chose me. I'll certainly do my best."

"I'm sure you will, Stan."

He stood up, all innocent ego and little-boy charm, and the invisible spotlight followed him as he left my office. Abby looked daggers at him, but he passed by, oblivious. He never even knew he had been a suspect.

Jack telephoned me at home that night, sounding a bit distracted. Or maybe discouraged. He had promised to let me know when they identified the body in the morgue, and they had. It was not Shirley Hastings at all but some poor girl from Toledo, a runaway who had frequented the singles bars on First Avenue. They were questioning the man she had picked up last Wednesday, and there was enough evidence to hold him.

I was relieved that it wasn't Shirley, and I asked if they had ever talked to her dentist.

Jack confirmed that they had. "We got her X-rays late this afternoon, but by then we already had a make on the body. We ran the dental check anyway, though, just to confirm that it wasn't Shirley."

"I wonder where she is, though," I said.

"We'll follow through when her parents get back from Canada," Jack said, "but I think we can almost eliminate her as a factor in Marcia's murder."

"You seem to have eliminated Editor John Terrific, too," I said.

"How do you know that?"

"I talked to Stan Ryden this afternoon, and he gave me his boyish lopsided grin and reeked of innocence."

"A real ham actor," Jack agreed. "But it seems quite definite that he hadn't the foggiest idea he had ever been mentioned for Marcia's job."

"On the other hand," I went on, "Nate Meyer was blustering all over the place, absolutely furious with you."

"Yes, he's full of *sturm* and *drang,* isn't he? What did he say to you?"

"He accused me of sicking you on him."

"I see. Why is it, Karen, that everybody talks about you when I go to question them? What are you telling them about me?"

"Nothing. Nothing at all. What do you think? But *I* can't make a move without being asked all about *you.* You should never have driven me home from the funeral Saturday."

"What's that got to do with anything?"

"Meredith Baker has a big mouth, that's what it's got to do with. And she and Joe Blackwell and Terry Kerman are broadcasting their speculations to the wide world."

"I see. That rather complicates things, doesn't it?"

"Well, between the murder and my supposed affair with you, there won't be any dull lunch conversations at the Italian Pavilion or Madrigal all week."

"I see."

There was a long pause, and I could almost hear his mind ticking.

"You are trying to figure out a way to use this," I accused him.

"It crossed my mind," Jack admitted. "But I wouldn't want to embarrass you."

"What about you in the police department?"

"What do you mean?"

"Are the cops talking about us, too?"

"Not that I know of. Anyway, I was figured as an oddball years ago. It's a useful reputation, lets me go pretty much my own way."

I sighed heavily, and Jack chose to misinterpret it.

"I'm sorry if this is embarrassing you."

He was repeating himself, and I could see there was no point in pursuing this line of conversation, so I got back to Nate.

"Did you find out where he was Monday night?"

"Who? What?"

"Nate Meyer. He said he wouldn't tell you where he had been the night of the murder."

"Now, why would he tell you that?"

"You mean it isn't true?"

"I didn't say that."

"Oh, stop being so cautious. Anyway, I figured out a way to find out where he was."

"Karen, you're asking for trouble, do you know that?"

"I've already got it, so what does it matter? Anyway, if you won't tell me, I'll go into his office and sneak a look at his desk calendar. He's so meticulous, he's sure to have jotted down what his plans were for last Monday."

There was kind of a strangled sound at the other end of the line, which resolved itself into laughter.

"You've already found out," I accused him. "You looked when you were in there today."

"No, better than that. I phoned his secretary later—while he was talking to you, probably—and she very obligingly checked for me. He has a standing commitment to Bellevue Hospital on Monday nights."

"Bellevue Hospital?"

"Yes. Nate Meyer, that arrogant blusterer, is doing volunteer work with handicapped children at Bellevue Hospital every Monday night."

"Including the night of the murder?"

"Including the night of the murder. One of the resident doctors said he stayed late, helping clean up after a puppet show."

"Nate Meyer?"

"Nate Meyer."

"What a fraud he is."

"Complete and absolute. Did he have anything else to say?"

I racked my brains "He's the first person I can think of who has said an unkind word about Marcia."

"What was that?"

"I'm trying to think how he phrased it. I think he didn't like the way she could manipulate George Griffith. Yes. That was it. He said she led George around like a poodle on a leash."

"So Nate noticed that. I wonder who else did."

"Well, *I* did, of course, but I don't think it was necessarily wrong of Marcia to handle the situation like that. She got things done, and she certainly protected the editorial department that way."

"And George Griffith didn't mind?"

"I don't think he ever realized."

"I wonder."

I pictured Jack with his inevitable notebook, jotting all this down, but I kept seeing him across the room at my desk, not all the way out

105

in Queens, in that unknown apartment in Jackson Heights.

"Well, Karen, I guess that just about does it. Unless you had a chance to talk to Terry Kerman today."

"I forgot about that completely."

"Tomorrow is all right."

"No, I mean I forgot to tell you that I had lunch with her today."

"That was quick work. What happened?"

"Why, she called me, first thing this morning. She wanted to pump me about you, thought I would have an inside view of what was going on in the case."

"Wheels within wheels. What did you tell her?"

"I said I thought it was unlikely that Joe Blackwell would come to trial for murder. That's all she cared about. She was afraid she'd have to testify, tell the world she had been with him that evening. And she thought that might wreck her new romance."

"I see."

"That was her secret—her new boy friend. I don't know if Joe knows about him, but she broke off with him—with Joe—the night of the murder. Did you know that?"

"Yes. He told me. That was what was so ironic. His wife didn't find out until it was all over."

"That's weird. I think they both blame you for nearly wrecking their marriage. Do you know that?"

"I didn't have a thing to do with it. I wasn't even the messenger that brought the bad news."

"No, Jack, you just happened to be around when it all came out."

"Can't be helped. Anyway, maybe if they can both blame me, they'll have a little less blame for each other."

"You're too philosophical by half. Joe is on the edge of being mad at *me,* too. He doesn't like it that I knew about him and Terry. And I suppose eventually Terry will be sorry she told me, too."

"Now you know how the police feel, being unloved most of the time."

"Doesn't it get lonely out there?"

"Frequently. But I'm not going to worry about that right now. It's late, and I'm tired."

"So am I."

"I'm sorry I kept you so long, Karen. I'll probably see you Thursday at the memorial service. Would you rather I ignored you? Would that make things easier for you?"

"I doubt it. Let's just see what happens. I don't really mind all the talk. It's just that I wish you would hurry up and solve this case. If I'm going to be paired off with a cop, at least he ought to be a *smart* cop."

"I'm working on it."

"I'm glad to hear it. Good night, Jack."

"Good night, Karen. And please be careful. You're complicating my life enough as it is."

I hung up thoughtfully. Now what do you suppose he meant by that?

I was having lunch the next day at San Marino with Leroy Langner, the boring marketing director of MSI, when I happened to spot Meredith Baker hurrying in, obviously late. She saw me, too, and she gave a half salute as she sat down at a table with three men I didn't know. Two minutes later all three of them turned around and stared at me. I wouldn't have needed to pay a penny for the thoughts of any of them. In the frequent pauses in my conversation with Leroy—and talking with Leroy is always more pause than conversation—I deliberately gazed around the room. More often than not, I caught retreating glances, even from strangers. I'm getting paranoid, I thought; or if I'm not, maybe I should be. Only Nate Meyer, sitting two tables away with his back toward me, seemed oblivious.

But of all the people in the restaurant, it was only Nate who stopped to say hello on his way out. He introduced me to his lunch guest, too, who turned out to be Dick Frazier, the copywriter from Coleman, Kressman, and Yates.

"We're exploring a whole new direction for Readers' Circle ads," Nate said. "I expect you to hate it."

"You mean you're really going to go ahead with that idea to quote from sexy books?" I said. "We'll wind up with the first X-rated ads in the book-club business."

Dick Frazier shifted uncomfortably. "No, no, nothing like that. I was wrong about that. This is just a new way to personalize membership. With a chance to participate in—"

Nate turned on him with seeming ferocity. "I told you to let *me* handle this, Dick. Never tell editors anything ahead of time. Give them a *fait accompli* and they can't do anything but scream. It saves a lot of bother all around."

"It was a happy day for me, Nate, when they took you off MSI." I looked over at Leroy, and even he looked better by comparison. He had finally managed to figure out the waiter's tip so he could sign his American Express slip.

"Oh, who wants happiness?" Nate said. "Challenge is the thing. Get your detective to solve this murder, Karen, and maybe I can pull strings to get you promoted to managing editor of RC. Then we can have some really satisfactory fights." He turned to Dick. "Karen isn't anything at all like Marcia Richardson. You always know where you stand with her."

Dick just looked uncomfortable. And Leroy, slow as molasses, carefully returned his American Express card, with today's receipt, to his wallet, so we could finally get up and get out of there.

Nate and Dick followed us back along 53rd Street, and I could hear Nate describing Lieutenant Morrison as a "particular friend" of Karen's. "He is gathering together a choice collection of red herrings," Nate said, "and he is even investigating me." The sound of his laughter infuriated me.

It was on the tip of my tongue to say that Jack knew all about Nate's secret life at Bellevue Hospital, but I held back. It would only confirm Nate in his opinion that Jack was my "particular friend." What an obnoxious phrase!

Dick turned off at Lexington Avenue, glad to get away from us, and Nate yelled after him, something about the memorial service the next day. I refused to be drawn into another fight, and it was an excruciatingly long walk back to the Berwyn Publishing Company and Rockefeller Center.

The only interesting phone message I had was that Harry Richardson had called. I got hold of him at his office, between dental patients, and he was apologetic about disturbing me, particularly to ask me to do him a favor.

I braced myself, sure that we were going to wind up talking about Jack Morrison, but that wasn't it at all. Harry had some difficulty getting to the point, but eventually I figured out that he had decided not to come to the memorial service for Marcia next day. There would be all those people in publishing, he said, and it would be awkward, and after all he had gone to the funeral in Philadelphia, and of course it was only right that he should have gone to Philadelphia, and he very much admired Mrs. Underwood, and he thought it was important for the family—even the ex-family—to rally around, and his sister from Scranton had been sorry that she couldn't come, too, but her husband's parents had been in Scranton for a visit, and they were elderly, and I thought he would never get to the point.

"And so, Karen—" he had finally wound up for the pitch—"I wonder if you would mind taking Tim and Hank with you. The boys are quite fond of you, you know, and of course they should be there to hear the tributes to their mother. They decided not to go back to camp until next week; they thought it was important to stay for this."

"Sure, Harry. I'll be glad to take them."

He gave me the address of his apartment, and I said I'd be there in a taxi at 1:00 P.M. The service was scheduled for 1:30 at Alice Tully Hall in Lincoln Center, and we would make it in plenty of time.

"I'll call George Griffith's secretary," Harry said. "There will be a special place reserved for the three of you. And thank you, Karen. This is really the best way to handle the situation, I'm sure."

Well, all that was easy enough. I made a note on my calendar for next day and was starting to draft a memo on the new mystery I had just bought from Putnam when I got a phone call from my cousins in Massachusetts. I had had a long-standing invitation to spend the next weekend with them breathing in the clean country air of the Berkshires and fending off the attentions of their neighbor down the road. He is a real-estate agent, and every year he gets richer and more boring. But luckily he isn't around all that much—summer weekends are busy times in the real-estate business. And anyway, I am really very fond of my cousins. We confirmed the time my bus would arrive, and I hung up the receiver thinking about something besides the murder and the office for a change. Actually, it wasn't all that much better: the laundry. Since I was going to be packing Thursday night, that meant I'd have to trundle my dirty clothes to the laundromat after work today. Life is so complicated by trivia. Washing and ironing we lay waste our powers. Wordsworth didn't know the half of it.

7

Tim and Hank and I arrived early at Alice Tully Hall next day. Even so, the place was already full. We identified ourselves and were ushered to aisle seats in the very first row—for one awful minute I thought we were going to be on the stage, but we had been spared that.

On stage already were George Griffith, presiding for the book clubs; Stan Ryden, representing the rest of the Berwyn Publishing Company; somebody from the corporate structure of Phoenix Industries; a man in a clerical collar; and a young woman in a long dress. Tim and Hank knew her: she had lived in their building and was a student at Juilliard—a very good soprano, it turned out.

We were seated in the same row with the corporate brass from Berwyn. I nodded at Barry Tremont, and when he whispered to the man next to him— the company treasurer, I think it was—I knew I was being identified. The boys were my only excuse for being in such fast company.

Behind us were the book-club editors—Joe Blackwell was two rows back, with Jack Morrison right next to him. Well, that was a good idea: Joe could identify anyone Jack needed to know. The rest of the auditorium was filled with a conglomeration of Berwyn people, agency representatives, and half the editors in town. It looked like the last presentation ceremony of the National Book Awards.

I spotted Meredith Baker in the middle of a small commotion in a side aisle. She was just arriving and was indignant that she didn't have a reserved seat. I slouched down where I was, unwilling to be evicted (I wouldn't have put it past her), and eventually somebody got up and gave her a place.

111

The service itself lasted about forty minutes and managed to be dignified and only slightly ponderous, and that was when the Phoenix Industries man was droning through the clichés prepared for him by his public-relations assistant. But George was brisk, and his remarks were sincere without being maudlin; and Stan submerged his own star quality in a surprisingly graceful tribute. Tim clutched at my hand at one point when Stan was reminiscing about the time Marcia came to his rescue at an autographing party (Tim explained later that he had been there, too), but otherwise the boys sat through the service composed, heads high, sustained by a quiet pride in their mother's memory. Marcia would have been proud of *them,* too.

Then George Griffith thanked us for coming, and it was all over. George and Stan greeted the boys, and I made introductions to the various Berwyn officers who stepped forward. I could see Joe Blackwell talking earnestly to Jack, presumably identifying the spectators. But the crowd thinned out in five minutes, everyone rushing off for taxis and buses back to midtown. Hank and Tim broke away temporarily and returned with Jack, who feigned reluctance at seeing me. (I *hoped* it was only feigned.) George Griffith's reluctance was genuine, though, and he was barely civil as he introduced Jack to the small circle of corporate executives who were still there.

"Are you going back to the office, Karen?" George inquired. "We can give you a lift."

"I'll be there in half an hour, George," I replied. "I have to take Hank and Tim home first."

"Jack is taking us in his police car," Hank piped up.

It was news to me, but Jack shrugged, as much as to say that it wasn't his idea, either. George stared disapprovingly at both of us. At any rate, Meredith wasn't there to look wise and knowing.

Considering the mob waiting for taxis, Hank and Tim and I were lucky to have transportation laid on by the New York City police department. The boys sat with Jack in the front seat, and he devoted his attention to them exclusively all the way to 89th Street. I saw them to the door there, and Jack waited while we said our good-bys.

He reached over to open the car door for me, and I slid into the seat beside him, both of us feeling a little subdued after the service, and a little awkward with each other, too.

I finally asked him how he was coming with the case, just to be polite and break the silence, but his head was someplace else, and I had to repeat the question to get his attention.

He was programmed to say they were doing some checking and following up some leads, but he caught himself, and his voice was rueful. "It's a bitch, Karen. All this information, all these people, and I know I'm missing something. I got off on the wrong foot, somehow, with the wrong mind-set. That sounds like foot-in-mind disease, doesn't it? But you know what I mean. Damn it, you *always* know what I mean. Maybe if you weren't in the picture and I could just step back far enough from the situation . . ."

He had veered to a sudden stop, right in front of the entrance to the Berwyn Building, and the taxi pulling up behind us had to brake sharply, with a squeal of tires. The cab driver would have yelled at us, except that we were police. And of course his passengers turned out to be George Griffith and Stan Ryden and Barry Tremont.

Jack recognized them, too. "Oh, hell. Your loquacious friends again. Well, let's really give them something to talk about." He leaned over and kissed me, with more enthusiasm than was strictly called for if he were acting, and I came out of it more than a little breathless.

"You want to slap my face?" Jack asked. "Is our audience still there?"

"No, they're retreating toward the revolving doors. You'll excuse me if I don't flounce out immediately. The last thing I want to do is ride up in the elevator with all of them."

"I'll excuse you. And I'm sorry if I embarrassed you, Karen. But the temptation was irresistible."

He didn't look sorry at all.

A second taxi drew up and discharged some Berwyn magazine editors, but unfortunately Jack did not know them and did not feel constrained to repeat his performance.

"Will you be in town this weekend, Karen?"

"No, I'm going to Massachusetts." I did not elaborate on that, and he did not pursue it. He didn't look disappointed, either. He just leaned past me to open the door, and he patted my shoulder as I slid out. He was whistling as he drove away, and he looked as self-satisfied at that moment as Stan Ryden does all the time. All that was missing was the lopsided smile.

I did not stir out of my office the rest of the afternoon, and I concentrated full force on the newest mystery from Scribners. It's amazing how much you can get done if you refuse to let yourself be distracted.

Elly Crawford dropped by that night while I was packing, and I gave her the duplicate key to my mailbox for the weekend.

"I'm leaving directly from the office," I explained, "and I'll probably be back early Sunday evening. It depends on the weather. If it's really glorious up there, I'll take the last bus back."

I dumped out the contents of my black pocketbook and switched most of the stuff to my white straw bag. The sheet of paper with Jack's phone number fell on the floor and Elly picked it up curiously.

"Have you seen him again? He didn't get in touch with me about the horoscopes, and I hoped he would. Has he solved the case yet?"

"Not yet, Elly. But he's working on it."

"Do you think I should call and ask him for the birth dates?"

"No, I wouldn't do that. I don't really think he believes in astrology."

She was clearly disappointed. "Well, maybe I could sort of work on it on my own. Like, do you know when Marcia's birthday was?"

"Oh, Elly, please don't get involved. The case is complicated enough as it is."

"I'm only trying to help."

I felt an echo of my own frustration for the past week, and I relented. Besides, why shouldn't Jack be pulled in as many directions as I was? It would serve him right.

"All right, Elly. If you insist. But if he growls at you, don't blame me."

She nodded happily and stuffed the paper in the pocket of her blue jeans. With any luck, she'd forget it.

The Friday editorial meeting went off smoothly next morning, and then Joe disappeared into George Griffith's office. There was a deadline coming up in Readers' Circle, and Joe would need clearance to buy the next club selection—he was enthusiastic about a Civil War novel from Harcourt Brace.

He reappeared fifteen minutes later, looking like a thundercloud. He closeted himself briefly with Jerry Goulden in the office next to mine, and then both he and Jerry came into my office and closed the door.

"We've got trouble," Joe said, almost unnecessarily.

I looked at him expectantly, and Jerry sat down while Joe paced.

"George says I can't buy any selections for RC unless I have the full concurrence of an advisory committee."

"He pulled that a year ago," I said, "and somehow Marcia talked him out of it. Actually, what I think she did was say that *you* were her advisory committee and the two of you would always be unanimous in any decision you made."

Joe nodded grimly. "Yes. But George isn't buying that now. He says that when he appoints a new editorial director—and he is not prepared to name one yet—he may return to that system. But while I'm managing editor, I have to appoint a committee, to be approved by him. Actually, he suggested the members of the committee to me, and I'm supposed to accept them unless I have any overriding reason not to. If I disagree, we'll have another meeting Monday to haggle over that." Joe shook his head. "And in the meantime the Book-of-the-Month Club judges are reading that Civil War novel for their meeting Tuesday, and the Literary Guild is prepared to make some kind of offer, and if we want to stay in the ball game we have to be cleared to bid, too."

"Won't they hold off the bidding if you ask?"

"No, it was a simultaneous submission, and we've had just as much time as BOM and Guild."

"I see. Well, who does Joe want on the committee?" I asked.

"You, and Jerry, and Rachel MacDowell, and either John Lomond or Beth Harris."

Rachel edits the Biography Book Club, John has the Science Club, and Beth has Movie Story.

"That's too many people," I said.

Joe agreed emphatically. "I told him that. I suggested that we split it in two, with two advisory editors for fiction and two for nonfiction."

"Will he buy that?"

"He wants a memo, Karen. And I want you to draft one for me. Right now. I've got a lunch date I can't break. And besides, you know Marcia's style. You can probably get around him."

"I'll try, Joe. But you had better leave my name out of this. I don't think George is very approving of me these days."

I thought of that scene in the police car yesterday, and Joe grinned, reading my mind. "George told me. He seemed more entertained than anything. All he said was that you didn't seem to be under any suspicion at all. At least, not for murder."

Jerry looked bewildered, but I had no doubt that Joe would enlighten him.

I sighed and pulled out a yellow pad to make notes. "All right, Joe. Who do you want on the two committees?"

"Jerry and Rachel for nonfiction, you and Beth for fiction. We'll leave John out of this. He's great on science, but his tastes are too academic for RC."

I silently agreed.

"The thing is, Karen," Joe went on, "it means that you will have to read the book over the weekend so we can all discuss it Monday morning."

"And Beth?" ˙

"Don't you remember? She was first reader on it and loved it. That's half the reason I took it home myself."

"And the other half?"

"Harcourt is pushing it like mad. A fifty-thousand first printing. So you better like it, too, Karen." For the first time in ten days the bantering tone was back in his voice and he sounded a little bit like his old self.

"What a farce all this is," Jerry said, turning to Joe. "Doesn't George know that you'll be able to get agreement from your advisory committee on anything you really want? When did you ever disagree with Marcia on selections?"

Joe considered that carefully. "Oddly enough, I think we were usually in complete agreement. In four years there were only two times that I can think of—no, three—when there was any dispute at all. Usually by the time we had both read everything and considered the schedule and the money and what was available, all the arrows pointed in one direction. And we'd try to get the runners-up for alternates. When we disagreed, it was about marginal books. Anyway, there's no point in looking back. Whatever problems we had in the past, we worried about then. There's always a new crisis for the next deadline."

"I suppose so." But I saw it more as an invasion of my time than as a crisis. "How big is this manuscript I have to cart away for the weekend?"

"Two boxes' worth," Joe said. "More than six hundred pages. Tell Abby to get it from my office. No, I'll tell her myself. You start work on the memo."

I groaned and rolled a couple of sheets of paper into my typewriter while Joe and Jerry departed for lunch. Abby obligingly brought me back a sandwich from the cafeteria and stuck around to make a clean copy from my rough draft: The Formation of a Temporary Editorial Advisory Committee.

I wondered how temporary it would be.

George Griffith came back from lunch before Joe returned, and he wandered into my office looking for him.

"He was supposed to write me a memo," George complained. "Or did he delegate that to you?" he said, spotting the Xerox copy on my desk. He picked it up and read through it, without expression.

"Sounds just like Marcia," he said. "Just like her postscript memos."

I had no idea that he had ever heard the phrase, but he seemed to ignore any pejorative meaning in the words.

"That's fine," George said, and I didn't realize how tense I had been until I relaxed after his compliment.

"You can tell Joe he can go ahead on this basis," George said, sitting down. "No postscripts will be necessary ever again, I hope. I want you to know, Karen, that I'm going to be making some changes in the way the editorial department is organized."

The tension came back all over again.

"I've talked to Joe about this," George continued, "and I've explained that we have to broaden the base of decision-making."

117

"The thing is," I began tentatively, "there's often a problem of time. And when you get a committee system . . ."

"We'll work that out," George said brusquely.

I seethed quietly. If he wanted to get a committee into MSI, too, I'd quit; I really would.

"Now, Karen," George said, contriving to look down at me even though we were both sitting down, "I want you to tell me how this murder investigation is proceeding."

It was a question that caught me by surprise. "I don't really know," I floundered. "The police don't seem to have a handle on it yet."

"Most unfortunate," George said. "You realize that I must delay the editorial reorganization until this case is resolved."

"Why?"

"Surely that is obvious. Imagine the repercussions if someone on the staff had really played any part in this crime."

"But I thought you were convinced that we are all innocent."

"Oh, I am. *I* certainly am convinced. But that doesn't necessarily mean that the police would agree. I don't know what kind of wild-goose chase they have embarked on."

And so you're pumping me to find out, I thought.

"Well," I said, trying to choose my words with care, "it seems to me that the staff has been pretty well cleared of suspicion."

"That's what your detective friend tells you?"

I could feel myself starting to blush. "No, that's what I gather just from talking to everybody. They can all account for their whereabouts last Monday night." It occurred to me to wonder where George had been then. And I wondered if Jack would tell me if I asked him.

Joe rescued me from further floundering by appearing in my doorway, holding the original of my memo on the advisory committee. He seemed surprised to see George and looked at me questioningly.

I could only shrug.

"Yes, I've read it," George said, interpreting all this body language with no trouble at all. "It's all right to go ahead on the basis of the two committees."

"I would have written the memo myself, George," Joe explained, "but time was pressing, and I had a lunch date I couldn't get out of."

George brushed that aside as of no consequence. "Always delegate

118

as much as you can, Joe. That may have been Marcia's one failing. She took too much on herself." He got up to leave and paused in the doorway.

I braced myself for some crack about that scene in the police car yesterday, but he evidently thought better of it and departed without another word.

Joe looked after him speculatively and waited until he was out of sight before he came in. "Did he give you a bad time?"

"Not really. Except I don't like this idea of completely reorganizing the editorial department. What does he mean by that?"

"Damned if I know. I don't like it either. And he still hasn't said a word about whether I'll get the top job."

"Sometimes I think there's a streak of sadism in George T. Griffith."

"What does the T stand for?"

"I don't know. Tecumseh?"

"Tyrant."

"Traitor."

"Tantalizer."

"Tempter."

"That's the same thing."

"It is not."

Abby came in, bearing the two-box manuscript, and looked at us as if we had lost our marbles. "I don't know what game you're playing, but it's not up to your usual standards."

"Well, it's been a hard week," I said. "And the weekend doesn't look so great, either. Do you know I have to lug that thing all the way to Massachusetts?"

"It goes fast," Joe said consolingly.

"Maybe if I start right now, I can get through a hundred pages and lighten the load," I said.

That remark was taken as a hint, and they both cleared out. And I actually got through all of Part I before I packed up and left to catch the bus.

The weather was great in the Berkshires that weekend, my cousins were full of family news, the concert at Tanglewood was all Mozart,

119

the real-estate agent was richer and only marginally more boring than last year, and the Civil War novel stayed readable all the way to Appomattox (I finished it on the bus coming back). But there was a grayness to all the time anyway. I missed Lieutenant Jack Morrison every waking minute.

I didn't hear from him again until Monday afternoon at the office. He called to complain that Elly Crawford had phoned him to ask for Marcia's birth date, and Harry's, too, and his girl friend's, if there was one.

"What did you tell her?"

"I actually gave her Marcia's dates—I had her file right in front of me at the time. But I said I didn't know the others. And then she wanted to know if it was all right if she called Harry to ask him. I discouraged her as firmly as I could, but she's so flaky I don't know what she's going to do. You know some really weird people, Karen."

"I guess so."

"What's the matter? You don't sound like yourself."

"I'm OK. We're having some problems in the office, that's all. George is going to reorganize things, but he's waiting until you solve the murder, so we're all in a state of suspended animation. Making any progress?"

"Only negatively. One bit of good news, though."

"What?"

"Shirley Hastings is OK. She got back to Massapequa yesterday with her family. She was in Canada all along."

"How did you find out?"

"Mrs. Dimaria. You remember her aunt, Mrs. Dimaria?"

"How could I forget?"

"Yes, of course. Well, in that phone conversation last week Mrs. Dimaria mentioned that the family would probably be back this week-end. So I phoned last night and asked for Shirley, and there she was. She hadn't known a thing about the murder and was shocked to hear about it. I asked her about Ricardo, too."

"What did she say?"

"It seems she broke off with him when she realized he was into something criminal, and then she got scared. She doesn't know anything concrete, unfortunately, so she can't be a witness if we ever get him to trial. But anyway, that's why she stopped seeing him, got herself fired from her job, and moved out of her apartment. She didn't want him to find her. She's going to apply for unemployment insurance today, by the way."

I had forgotten he was going to run a check on that.

"You seem to be eliminating suspects right and left," I said.

"Yes. We finally—" He broke off abruptly and I could hear someone calling to him in the background. "I have to hang up now, Karen. Talk to you later."

Abby buzzed me to say that Elly had called while I was on the phone with Jack. Her message was that she thought she had solved the murder and she would tell me tonight. So I supposed she had phoned Harry and his birthday had been incriminating. Poor Harry, born under the wrong stars. I wondered how she had persuaded him to give her his dates. He didn't even know her.

Abby brought in the afternoon mail and asked me what Elly could possibly know, and together we scoffed at the whole astrology scene.

"But will she *do* anything?" Abby asked. "Will she go over to his apartment and confront him or anything like that?"

"I can't imagine it," I said. "And anyway, even if she did, Harry would only laugh, I'm sure. Or maybe call the police and have her thrown out."

"So you're convinced that Harry is innocent," Abby said.

"Sure."

"But it would be really strange, wouldn't it, if she had accidentally stumbled onto the real killer. Who do you suppose it is, Karen?"

I had spent half the weekend worrying that question, and I had a new favorite suspect to replace the lawyer, Ted Ferris. Jack hadn't mentioned Ferris for days, which wasn't necessarily conclusive, but probably meant he was not a prime suspect. No, my new candidate was the president of the book clubs, none other than George T. Griffith. The more I thought about it, the more I liked the idea. George was tired of being led around by the nose by Marcia, he kept asking me leading questions about how the investigation was going, he knew her unlisted phone number, he was jittery in that conversation after the agency review. . . .

121

"Karen, I asked you who you think the murderer is," Abby repeated plaintively.

"I don't want to name anyone at this point," I said. "I don't think the police have settled on anyone yet, either."

"What did Jack say when he called?"

"He was talking about Elly and astrology and . . . Good grief! I forgot to tell you the most important news of all. Jack talked to Shirley Hastings last night. She's back in Massapequa with her parents. She was on that trip through Canada with them, and she didn't know a thing about the murder."

"Oh, I'm so relieved, Karen. I didn't want to tell you, but there was a news story in the *Times* the day we were trying to find her, the day I talked to her aunt. The police found some poor girl's body in a car in Brooklyn, and I had the most horrible premonition that it was Shirley. Wouldn't that have been awful?"

I nodded. We were all secret detectives.

"And then," Abby went on, "it turned out that the girl was killed by that insurance man she picked up in a singles bar. The most unlikely people turn out to be murderers. It makes you distrust everybody, doesn't it?"

"It certainly does."

Abby lingered in front of my desk, unwilling to let the conversation die. "Karen, you didn't ask me who *I* think killed Marcia."

"Who?"

"Stan Ryden. Don't laugh—I mean it. Everybody is taken in by that little-boy grin of his, but he's sneaky, Karen; he really is."

"But Abby, why would *he* be involved? Why would he want to kill Marcia?"

"Because Mr. Griffith is going to bring him in as editorial director of the book clubs. You just wait and see. Why else would he have Stan speak at the memorial service for Marcia? It should have been Joe Blackwell up there on the stage. We were all talking about it afterward, Karen, all the secretaries. It wasn't right to have Stan there instead of Joe. Joe worked with her and knew her best of all of us. It just wasn't right that he didn't speak. It wasn't fair."

She had a point, and I had wondered about it, too, but I gave her my rationalizations. "I think George was there to represent the book

122

clubs; that's the way he saw it. And he brought Stan in to represent the rest of the Berwyn Company. I don't think it was a willful put-down of Joe." Or maybe it was, at that. There's something sadistic about the way George plays with people.

"You can think that if you want to," Abby said, "but Joe is getting a dirty deal in all of this. If they bring Stan in, he ought to quit. We all ought to quit, just to show them."

"Abby, calm down. It hasn't happened. I don't really think it will. The problem is that we'll probably all drag along in this state of uncertainty until the police solve the case."

"When will that be?"

"I wish I knew."

"Well, Karen, you just tell Jack to investigate Stan Ryden. You can get him to do that, can't you? I bet he'd do anything you asked him."

"My influence on Jack Morrison is considerably less than everybody thinks."

"I don't believe that. I heard about Thursday, right here in front of this building."

"That was his idea of a joke."

Abby looked skeptical, but she refrained from further comment. Instead, she scooped up the contents of my Out Box and headed for the door. "All the same, Karen, you ask him to investigate Stan Ryden."

I played, fleetingly, with the idea of George and Stan conspiring at murder, but I simply couldn't believe that one, either.

Maybe it wasn't anybody we knew at all. Maybe it was a burglar who simply wanted to read Marcia's long-neglected novel and couldn't find it at his local library. If Jack didn't dream up another reason to come see me, I'd have to ask him if I could borrow the book.

8

I was half expecting Elly to be waiting for me when I got home, but she wasn't there and her mailbox was still full.

Eddy Palmieri, her boy friend, phoned me a little after seven o'-clock, impatient and self-important, as always.

"Karen, Elly was supposed to meet me at six thirty in Paley Park, and she's not here yet. What happened?"

"I don't know, Eddy. She didn't come home, and I haven't talked to her. Could she be working late?"

"I hope not. She's got a job with your ad agency this week. Did you know that? Would they keep her after seven at night?"

"I can't imagine it."

"Well, we were supposed to get a hot dog here and then go to a Zen lecture, and I'll be late if I can't leave in another ten minutes. I'm going on without her if she's not here by then. You tell her that in case she phones."

Crazy Eddy. This wasn't the first time he had relied on me to relay messages—Elly has a way of wandering off at the last minute when she sees destiny beckon. All the same, I started to worry.

It was foolish. She'd probably arrived in Paley Park two minutes after Eddy called. They were on their way to that Zen lecture right now. She'd be popping in later, after ten some time, full of the sound of one hand clapping and all that jazz. And ready to explain why Cancer is programmed to kill Capricorn, or whatever.

I worried just the same. Suppose she really *had* fingered the murderer. I couldn't remember if I had heard that Harry had a solid alibi for the Monday night Marcia was killed. Or his girl friend, either.

Suppose Elly walked in on the two of them together and accused them, and Harry reached for a gun. . . .

Harry isn't any murderer. Marcia's death was a shock to him, too, disrupting his marriage plans, for one thing.

His girl friend teaches home economics up in Riverdale, Jack said. Jean Ann Larrabee, her name is. Maybe she knows about household poisons and right now is concocting something deadly. Elly wanders in on the two of them with her wild theory, and this home-ec teacher smiles and offers to get her a drink. . . . But Elly never touches alcohol. A little marijuana maybe, but not alcohol. Perhaps you put arsenic in coffee or tea, though. In that Dorothy Sayers novel *Strong Poison,* the murderer contrived to have arsenic mixed up in an omelet. Elly doesn't like eggs. . . .

This is silly. I should call Jack and let him handle this. But when I tried phoning him, there was no answer.

Suppose Elly is there at Harry's right now. There ought to be some way to stop him. Perhaps if I telephoned . . . And then what? Maybe Harry is at home, innocent as can be, placidly paying bills or writing a letter to Hank and Tim at camp. What would I say? I know: I'll phone and ask for the boys' address and sort of casually find out if Elly phoned him today.

I dialed his number and counted ten rings. God, it was just like the night Marcia was killed, two weeks ago. I checked my watch—7:45 —remembering how fascinated the police are by exact times. I called twice more in the course of the evening, and Harry answered, finally, just before ten o'clock.

"Karen, how are you? I've been meaning to call and thank you for taking Tim and Hank to that service last week. They were both quite impressed. I understand that the editor from paperback books—what was his name?"

"Stan Ryden."

"Yes, Stan Ryden. I understand that he gave a very good talk, mentioned a party that Tim remembered."

"Yes, Stan gave a fine tribute. The whole service was done very well, I thought. Dignified. I was glad the boys could go."

"And thank you for taking them. What's on your mind?"

"I called to get their address at camp. There's just a chance I'll be

125

.

in Connecticut, or I might want to write to them, or something. By the way, Harry, I tried to reach you earlier this evening."

"I just got back. I was having dinner with a friend. I . . . I'll get you the address."

I wondered if he had been going to tell me about Jean Ann Larrabee and then thought better of it.

I took down the address carefully, Harry spelling out the Indian name twice.

And then I couldn't think of any graceful way to tell him about Elly, so I just plunged in.

"Harry, there's something else on my mind, too."

"Yes?"

"Harry, I've got this kind of kooky friend who is into astrology. Elly Crawford, her name is. She's got some kind of idea that she can figure out who killed Marcia by reading everybody's horoscope. Did she happen to telephone you today?"

"So *that's* what she was running on about."

"What?"

"My receptionist, Nancy Kennedy. She said a strange girl called her this morning, said she was making a survey, asked for her birthday, asked for my birthday, was quite persistent."

"What happened?"

"I'm not sure. I think Nancy gave the dates to her. It seemed to be the only way to get her off the phone."

We laughed at the absurdity of it all, and I said I hoped she wouldn't bother him again, and he thanked me again for taking care of Hank and Tim.

I hung up, considerably relieved. It was true that Elly hadn't come in yet, but that wasn't without precedent. It wouldn't be the first time she had stayed over with Eddy in the Village.

My clock radio went off at 7:30 next morning, as usual, and I lay in bed, drowsily debating whether to get up immediately or to drift back to sleep for another twenty minutes. The sleep won, as it almost always does, until I was shocked awake by the sudden jangle of the telephone. The last time an early-morning call woke me was two years ago, when my father phoned to say that Uncle Chris had died. Heart pounding, I reached for the receiver, and it was Jack, his voice urgent, full of alarm.

"Karen, are you all right? Are you safe?"

"Sure. I'm fine. A little sleepy—you woke me up. What's the matter?"

"Thank God. Now you just stay there. Don't leave the apartment. Don't let anybody in, even if you know him. *Particularly* if you know him. Do you understand?"

"Yes. No. I don't know. What are you talking about? What happened?"

"There's been another murder. Elly Crawford. I don't know what it's all about. They phoned me an hour ago—she was carrying my name and phone number in her pocketbook. I thought . . . But I've seen the body. It's Elly. I'm coming to see you right away. I'll be there in twenty minutes. Don't let anybody in until I get there. You're sure you're all right?"

"Yes, Jack, really."

I dressed with lightning speed, put on a pot of coffee, and had just finished making the bed when my doorbell rang. Whatever control I had had until then simply vanished, and I started to shake.

Jack pounded up the stairs and held me for a minute to make sure I was really all in one piece.

Then he checked the doors and windows—for a minute I thought he was going to look under the bed, too—and finally he sat down at my desk and pulled out his notebook and got a grip on himself.

"This makes no damned sense at all," he said.

My head was a mass of conflicting stresses, stray thoughts darting in and out, swifter than hummingbirds, and I couldn't catch one long enough to examine it. Elly is dead. Jack loves me. The coffee is going to boil over. Somebody is trying to kill me. Can it really be Harry? Who will tell Tim and Hank? It's all impossible. What *happened?*

"Now, Karen, we're going to review this step by step and . . . You have to pull yourself together, my dear. Maybe some coffee would help?"

"Coffee," I echoed, heading for the kitchen like a sleepwalker. But I dropped the first cup I reached for, and it shattered on the floor. I shattered with it, and Jack was there instantly, holding me, soothing me as if I were six years old, murmuring endearments that I would have treasured if only my mind could have sorted them out and made sense of them all.

Somehow, though, I was seated in the dining alcove, and Jack was there across from me, pouring coffee and talking some nonsense about our first breakfast together, and I felt the sobs subsiding and something like reason returning.

"I feel as if I've been through a typhoon," I said.

"So do I," Jack said. "Twice. But just now, the second time, it wasn't as bad as the first. The phone rang at six thirty, like an alarm bell in the night. I couldn't make any sense of what they were saying. For one horrible moment I thought it was you they meant. I think I would have gone a little crazy if it had been. Maybe I went a little crazy anyway. They looked at me very strangely when I got to the morgue."

"Then it's really true? Elly has been killed? What happened?"

"We don't know yet. Her body was discovered a couple of hours ago. In Carl Schurz Park, half hidden in some bushes. Some early-morning dog-walker . . ."

"In the park? But that's only a block away. There are people there all the time. Even at night it's safe." It was an article of faith with me. I'd been there often, heedless of the hour, always secure. Gracie Mansion, the mayor's residence, is right there, guarded by police twenty-four hours a day.

"That's where the body was found, Karen. She was strangled with a necktie, we think. Her purse was there, but her wallet was gone. There was other identification, though—some letters, an address book, that sheet of paper I had given you with my name and phone number. That's why they called me right away."

I explained how the paper had gone from me to Elly, and Jack just nodded.

"Someone is calling her family in Albany. And I suppose they are getting in touch with that boy friend of hers, Eddy."

"Yes. Eddy Palmieri. He called me last night. Elly was supposed to meet him at six thirty in Paley Park, but she still wasn't there half an hour later. I got worried about her, as a matter of fact. I called you, but you weren't home."

"No. I was following up something about Ted Ferris, Marcia's lawyer friend. We finally got hold of the doctor who treated him after he put his arm through a window up in Chatham."

"Yes?"

"Ferris is clear. All his time is accounted for, even without relying on the testimony of his new girl friend."

"I see."

"Why were you trying to reach me, Karen?"

"I wanted to know if I should do anything about Elly. She had called me in the office yesterday afternoon and left a message that she had solved the murder. So when she didn't show up to meet Eddy, I sort of panicked. I thought she might have gone to see Harry Richardson on her own."

"Harry Richardson?"

"Well, she really believed in that astrology stuff, and it turned out that she got his birth date and sign and all that. I thought maybe she had deduced something and then gone along to confront him, maybe in the presence of his girl friend."

"So what did you do after you called me?"

"I called Harry, and he wasn't home. So I kept calling, and finally he answered, said he'd been out for dinner. We had a very pleasant conversation, actually. He talked about the memorial service, and I asked him for the boys' address at camp. That was my excuse for calling, you see."

"I see. And then you asked about Elly?"

"Yes. And he said his receptionist had had a call from a strange girl who was very persistent about checking on their birthdays, so he thinks the receptionist told Elly. But he laughed about it, and I decided Elly hadn't been to see him and everything was OK. Probably she had found Eddy after all and gone to the Zen lecture with him, and so I stopped worrying. Did I do anything wrong?"

"No, I don't think so. We'll check out Eddy, of course. Do you know if he knew Marcia?"

"No. Elly didn't know her, either. Do you think the two murders are related?"

"I don't know what to think. But when they called me at six thirty this morning and said they had another body, and the address was the same as yours . . . You see, it struck me that Elly might have been killed by mistake. Maybe the murderer was really after *you.*"

"But why? Who would want to kill *me?*"

"I don't know. Possibly you've said something that makes him think you know who he is. Or you have a piece of information that will clear things up if you put it in the right perspective."

I racked my brains, but I couldn't imagine what it could be. Of course I *had* been talking to all those people at the office, and who knew what I might have let slip? And even if I hadn't said it—whatever *it* was—directly to the murderer, maybe it got back to him through someone else. Stan Ryden, in all innocence, could have told George Griffith . . . what? But all those people know me. They wouldn't confuse me with Elly.

I pointed out that difficulty to Jack.

"Did anyone in your office know Elly at all?"

"I don't think so. No, wait. I had a party for the editors last year, and Elly dropped in to borrow something and stayed five minutes. But I don't see how that could count, do you?"

"It's all such a maze. It gets harder and harder to rule anyone out. Even Harry Richardson."

"Where *was* he the night Marcia was killed?"

"With Jean Ann Larrabee, he says. And she does, too. They were having dinner. Nobody remembers them at the restaurant, but Harry has a Diners Club slip for that day."

"It might have been lunch instead of dinner."

"He had patients booked right through. He says he took out half an hour for a sandwich, and his records bear him out. So do his patients."

"Well, then, an early dinner and then the murder afterward."

"The timing is tight, going by your phone calls, but it's barely possible. I don't believe it, though."

"Neither do I."

"It's just that I can't rule it out positively."

"Abby, my secretary, thinks it's Stan Ryden. She says that George is going to name him editorial director and that's why he did it. She wanted me to make sure that you checked him out."

"We did. He's clear, too."

"And that leaves my candidate, George Griffith." I gave him my reasons, and Jack didn't say anything for a long minute.

Then he shook his head and stood up. "Karen, don't talk to anyone about this today. And steer clear of Griffith, just as a precaution." He looked at his watch, and involuntarily I looked at mine, too. It was after nine o'clock, and I would be later than usual.

"I suppose you'll be safe enough at the office. Who are you having lunch with?"

"I don't remember."

"Well, try to go out with at least two people. Or don't go out at all. Keep Abby with you."

"This is going to be very strange."

"Just be careful. I'll drive you to work. And pick you up afterward." He sighed ruefully. "What a mess. And we'll be back on the front pages for sure, now. A girl's body in Carl Schurz Park, in the mayor's own backyard."

I locked the door carefully as we left, and Jack glanced up the stairs at the door of Elly's apartment.

"Do you want to go in? I have the key."

"Not now. I'll be back with the lab boys in an hour or so There may be some indication of a hasty departure or a struggle or something. I don't want to disturb anything."

"But she didn't come home from work," I said. "Her mail was still in her mailbox." We paused on the ground floor and peered at the row of boxes. "See? It's still there."

"You mean to say Elly wasn't home yesterday when she was making those calls to you and to me and to Harry about checking the signs of the zodiac?"

"No. She takes part-time jobs, didn't I tell you? Eddy said she was working for our ad agency yesterday."

"*Your* ad agency. What did he mean by that?"

"I don't know. I didn't think about it. There's the Berwyn Advertising Agency, of course. But they use it just to promote Berwyn trade books and paperbacks. Each of the book clubs contracts with an outside agency. Maybe he meant that Elly was working for the agency doing campaigns for MSI. That's Lothrop and Logan. You know, I told you about the agency review last week."

"Lothrop and Logan. Yes." He unlocked the door for me, and he paused on the sidewalk to look around. I couldn't see anything suspicious, and I guess he didn't, either.

We had reached the office before he spoke again. "Karen, I'll meet you for lunch. I don't know exactly what time it will be, but I'll come up to your office and collect you. All right?"

"Yes."

"Be careful." He reached for my hand. "You know I love you."

"Yes. And I—"

But he cut short my declaration by honking the horn abruptly. He had spotted Abby hurrying toward the entrance of the Berwyn Building. She turned around and saw us and came over to the car and leaned in.

"Hi, Karen. You're as late as I am. Hi, Jack." She looked at him curiously and probably made all the wrong deductions.

"Abby," Jack began, "I'm going to tell you something in confidence. I don't want you to tell anyone else, even if you read all about it in the *Post* this afternoon."

"All right."

I opened the door and she got in the car with us while Jack told her about Elly's murder. "We don't know if Karen is in danger, Abby," he explained. "I don't really think so. On the other hand, I wish you would stick pretty close to each other today. Will you do that?"

"Of course. Do you mean to say you suspect somebody here at Berwyn?" She looked at me significantly, and I knew she was thinking of Stan Ryden.

"Not necessarily, Abby," Jack said. "It's just that we want to be cautious until we get this thing resolved. So don't go off playing detective, either of you. And if anything happens, anything at all, reach for the telephone."

But it was Jack who did the calling, and he reached me just before noon. He sounded exasperated, and he was. "We still haven't located Eddy. I don't think he went home last night. Do you have any idea where he might be?"

Eddy was casual about jobs and money and sleeping arrangements, to the point of irresponsibility, and it seemed to me that he could disappear anywhere. I was no help there at all.

"And we can't locate where Elly was yesterday, either," Jack went on. "Half the Berwyn Advertising Agency is out of the office for one reason or another, and the staff that's left behind has never heard of her. The office manager doesn't think they've hired anybody temporary this week, but she admits that sometimes an assistant is brought in directly by an account executive at the last minute and the papers are processed later."

"I don't know what to say, Jack."

"I tried Lothrop and Logan, too, but she wasn't there, either."

"Well, you could always check with Olsten's, I suppose. That's the temporary agency that sends her out on jobs."

"Good God. Why didn't you say so in the first place?"

"I don't know. I guess I thought you'd find out where she was by checking Berwyn directly. Eddy was just so offhand when he talked about 'your advertising agency' that it didn't register with me one way or the other."

"Yes, I see. We'll get on it right away. Everything else OK?"

"Yes. Except I can't concentrate on anything for two minutes running. I read the copy for the *MSI Bulletin* three times before it made sense to me. When are you coming?"

"Soon."

He was there within the hour, and we stood waiting for the elevator with Nate Meyer.

Jack greeted him, and Nate smirked at both of us. "Still investigating, Lieutenant?"

"That's my job," Jack said easily.

The elevator came, and we had it all to ourselves.

"And am I still under suspicion?" Nate asked.

"No, Bellevue gave you a clean bill of health. They said you had the best record of all the volunteers in the ward. Congratulations."

That caught Nate by surprise. "There's no privacy left in this world," he grumbled. "We might as well be living in a police state. And I suppose you'll blab it all over," he accused me.

"I doubt it. Nobody would believe me, anyway. You've worked too hard on your Mr. Hyde image to be a very credible Dr. Jekyll."

"That's it," Nate said. "Karen, I think you've hit on the key.

133

Lieutenant, you've got to find somebody who's working hard to look like Dr. Jekyll when he's been Mr. Hyde all along."

"One may smile, and smile, and be a villain," Jack said. "At least I'm sure it may be so in Denmark."

"Hey, you're supposed to do Yeats," I protested. "I thought it was your deputy chief inspector who quoted Shakespeare."

"Well, I sort of got into the act, too. Have to make a good impression on the boss, you know."

"A smiling villain," Nate said, obviously intrigued. "And would a half smile do as well? I wonder, Lieutenant, if you have gone beyond the book-club division in your search for suspects. Have you met Stan Ryden, for instance?"

"Nate, you're trying to sick Jack onto somebody else, exactly what you accused me of doing."

"Don't bother me with consistency, Karen." Nate followed us out of the elevator to the sidewalk. "I think you should look more carefully at the smiling Stan Ryden," Nate said. "He's on his way up in the world, and he doesn't care how he gets there."

"We're looking at everybody," Jack said. "But that doesn't give you a license to play detective, Mr. Meyer. This case has already been complicated by eager amateurs rushing in."

"It's just that the professionals don't seem to be making much headway," Nate shot back. "I think you need a little help."

We let him have the last word; and then Jack headed for a rather indifferent hotel restaurant that had one obvious advantage: there was nobody there we knew.

I decided that an omelet would be easier to swallow than anything else, and Jack ordered a steak sandwich.

"What's happening, Jack? Did you go back to Elly's apartment?"

"Yes. She lived a rather cluttered life, didn't she? But there was nothing there—at least on the surface—that gave us much help. I went over to Carl Schurz Park first, to see where the body had been found. The press was swarming all over the place."

"So it will be in the papers?"

"Yes. Page nine of the *Post* this afternoon. I bought an early edition, but I left it in the car. It doesn't say much, actually. And they haven't picked up the connection with Marcia's murder. The whole

134

thrust of the story is that the body was found in the mayor's own backyard, with policemen there within call."

I shook my head. "The murderer must be a really cold-blooded monster. And desperate, too. Do you really think the two crimes are related? You said her wallet was missing. Couldn't it have just been a mugging?"

"That's what Frank Reilly was trying to convince himself of, too. He talked to Harry Richardson at great length this morning, and we're sure that Harry is clean."

"But since Elly suspected Harry, why would someone else—the real murderer—try to kill her? It wouldn't do him any harm for her to go around accusing Harry."

"It doesn't make any sense," Jack repeated.

"But the two murders were so different—first a shooting and then a strangling."

"Yes. But neither one was planned far in advance. Both improvised. He's quick-witted, whoever he is."

"You keep saying 'he.' "

"I do, at that. But the English language is male chauvinist, haven't you noticed? Anyway, very few women have been stranglers."

"I don't see why Elly would ever go with him to some dark corner of the park—unless she knew him. That's really not like her at all."

"Well, once we pin down her movements yesterday, maybe we'll have some better idea of who it can be. We found out where she was working, finally. Olsten's said they had sent her to Coleman, Kress-man, and Yates."

"That's the agency for Readers' Circle."

"I remembered. We have two detectives there right now, talking to the staff. But almost everybody is out to lunch, so I don't think they can get much done for the next hour or so. It's a pity we lost the morning. I was so convinced we'd find her at the Berwyn Advertising Agency, right in the same building with all of you. The opportunities for implicating . . . somebody were so much better."

He was being evasive again.

"Jack, did you find out anything more about George Griffith?"

"More?"

"I told you I think he's been behaving kind of strangely."

"Yes, you did."

"Well?"

"Did it ever occur to you that he might think *you* are behaving strangely?"

I turned that over in my mind for a minute, with Jack watching me, his eyes practically dancing with wicked glee.

"You mean he accused me of murder?"

"Not in so many words, no. But the implication was there."

"Well, I think it's an outrage. George Griffith thinking that of me. The man is an idiot."

"No, I wouldn't say that. But he certainly doesn't understand women at all."

"And you do?"

"Well, better than he does. But that's not saying all that much. Karen, did you ever stop to think that his relationship with Marcia was quite peculiar? He treated her very differently from all the men who report directly to him—the business manager and the group marketing director and the production chief and all those people."

"Well, yes. But then he didn't have a clue about the way we operate, and I just thought he didn't understand editors."

"No, I think it's more than that. Now, for instance, he's behaving differently with Joe Blackwell. When there was a dispute about the temporary reorganization of the editorial department, he called Joe in and they talked about it. Then he asked for a memo from the editors —he didn't just send out something crazy on his own, a memo that would have to be corrected in a postscript later."

"Yes, you're right."

"I think that George Griffith simply doesn't know how to deal with women in a business situation. He sent out orders on paper and then pulled back as soon as Marcia raised any argument at all. He didn't know how to say no to her. He's going to be a lot more comfortable with Joe—if he chooses him, that is."

"Do you think he will?"

"Probably. He'll have to fight Barry Tremont to get Stan Ryden away from paperbacks, and I don't think Griffith has the stomach for that sort of thing. And anyway, from what you say, Joe Blackwell will do a first-class job. Why shouldn't Griffith take the path of least resistance?"

"I just wish he'd do it soon, though."

"I'll tell you one thing: he won't bring in a woman for the job."

"Male chauvinist pig."

"You may possibly have a point in this particular case."

"But could he have killed her?"

"I can't imagine it. George Griffith going willingly to Marcia's apartment for a confrontation when he couldn't even face her in the office?"

"No, I guess not. But that doesn't explain why he thinks *I* did it."

"But he doesn't understand *you,* either. He thinks you're very assured, competent, maybe after Marcia's job because you're so much like her."

"I *am?*"

"That's what's going on in *his* head. He also voiced some suspicions of Rachel MacDowell. He's just like Eddy Palmieri: *cherchez la femme.*"

"What does he have against Rachel?"

"Nothing concrete. The way Shirley was fired bothered him. It didn't bother Shirley—I asked her. And then I had another conversation with Rachel, too, but it turns out that she was actually relieved when Marcia took over that situation."

"Rachel didn't tell me you called her again."

"Not *every* suspect goes running to you, Karen. Anyway, it was relatively easy to disabuse George Griffith of his suspicions against Rachel, but he was persistent about you. You're a devious woman, he told me, and you went after me to divert suspicion. Quite a blow to my pride, thinking you didn't want me for myself alone."

"George Griffith is crazy, and I thought you were terrific from the first time I saw you. But you must know that, Jack."

"I sort of guessed."

We smiled at each other, and I floated free and said exactly what I was thinking: "Let's get married."

"Hey, slow down a minute. Isn't that my line?"

"Well, I was feeling liberated. But I'm generous: you can say it, too.

Anyway, you are sometimes so maddeningly slow about picking up cues that I just thought I'd skip ahead and save us both a lot of time."

"Karen, we met exactly two weeks ago today. And you were away one whole weekend of that time. Give me a little credit, my sweet. Look at all those reasons I invented for coming to see you."

"And look at all those excuses you made for dropping me at my doorstep before the coach turned back into a pumpkin."

"So you noticed that."

"Darling, how could I help it?"

"It seemed so logical at the time. I thought if we got too involved I wouldn't be able to think straight about clearing up this case." He had finished his coffee and signaled for the bill. "It didn't work," he went on ruefully. "I haven't cleared up the case, and there's another murder, too. I wanted a solution first, the whole thing wrapped up in ribbons to dazzle you and sweep you off your feet."

"That's a good script, too," I acknowledged. "How do we make it come out that way?"

Jack looked at his watch. "I think the next step is to get over to the agency, now that their extended lunch hour is almost over. Do you know anyone at Coleman, Kressman?"

"Just the copywriter Nate introduced me to last week. I don't go to RC agency reviews. Joe does, and Nate."

"Well, if necessary I'll call Joe later this afternoon. He's considerably more cooperative."

"Yes. He's the one who told me that Nate had a fight with the copywriter at the last review. Dick Frazier."

"Dick Frazier?"

"Yes. The copywriter, Dick Frazier. I told you there'd been a fight, about sex in the ads or something."

"But you never mentioned a name." Jack was leafing back through the pages of his notebook, checking on his interview with Nate, but the name wasn't there, either. "Dick Frazier," Jack said again. "I've heard it somewhere before. . . ." He had riffled all the way back to the beginning of his notebook before he found what he was looking for, and then his voice was triumphant: *"Forbidden Passion* by Richmond Frazier. That's the set of galleys Marcia was reading when she was killed."

"Good heavens, you're right. Richmond Frazier. Dick Frazier. I never made the connection. Well, that explains why she was reading it, anyway. It was such a ghastly book, all full of incest and graphic sex scenes. Marcia normally would have thrown it out on the basis of my report. I just assumed that the publisher must have pleaded with her as a special favor to take a look. So it was the author who pleaded with her instead."

"And that's all you see in this—an explanation of why she was reading that particular book?"

"Well, yes. I mean, it's sort of a coincidence that Dick Frazier works at our advertising agency. No, that's not coincidence; that's the reason. If she hadn't known him, she wouldn't have bothered."

"It's more than coincidence, and I've been an idiot," Jack said. "Chasing off after Marcia's book instead of concentrating on what she was reading at the time."

"But I've just explained it to you. It was perfectly natural for Marcia to look at the book, as a special courtesy to the copywriter at the agency. She had no quarrel with him. It was Nate who was fighting with Dick Frazier."

Jack shrugged that off as of no consequence. "Karen, who else would have known that Dick Frazier and Richmond Frazier are one and the same and that Marcia was reading those galleys?"

"Well, I suppose Joe Blackwell knew. He would have recognized Dick's name when the galleys came in. Nate doesn't see the list of submissions—he might not have known anything at all."

"I'll ask Joe. Do you think he read the book, too?"

"I don't know. Maybe. But if Marcia was just going to glance at it as a courtesy, he wouldn't have had to read it, too. I told you, *I* read it. It wasn't anything we would touch in a million years."

"Yes, so you said. What was it about? I mean, between the sex scenes, what was it about?"

"It was one of those growing-up novels, you know. There was this teen-age boy. And he was introduced to sex by his mother. A very strong woman—the incest was out of character for her. And then he got involved with his sister, who was sort of literary. And then he took on both of them at once. Really, it was too awful."

"Where was the father while all this was going on?"

139

"I don't remember exactly. He was sort of a vague figure, disappeared halfway through the book, went off to war or something. . . ."

My voice trailed off and I realized what I had said.

"Yes," Jack said. "It sounds familiar. It could be Marcia's novel, expanded with all those sex scenes. I think we're on to something. Now let me think this out. We have to be sure of our facts. Where can we get a set of those galleys?"

"Don't the police have the ones Marcia was reading?"

"Yes, but I don't want to use them. They're part of the evidence, and the bloodstains . . ."

"I see," I said hastily. "Well, the publisher probably sent us two sets. Let's go back to the office and see if the other galleys are on file."

"Right. And I still have the copy of Marcia's book, the one her mother let me borrow. You come home with me and we'll check out the book against the galley proof. I want to be absolutely sure."

Back at the office Joe Blackwell looked at us, bewildered, when I asked him for the duplicate copy of Dick Frazier's novel.

"Is he hounding *you* to read that, too? He pestered me after the agency review, and I read the first three chapters, but it was hopeless. Pretty close to pornography, I'd say."

"So you knew that Dick Frazier of the agency was really Richmond Frazier, the author?" Jack asked.

"Well, of course. That's why I felt I had to look at his book when he asked me. I told Marcia it was unnecessary for her to waste her time on it, but she said he phoned her and pleaded."

"I don't understand," Jack said, "why nobody told me that Dick Frazier of the agency was the author of the book Marcia was reading when she was killed."

"It didn't seem relevant," Joe said. And from the tone of his voice, he obviously still felt the same way. He looked at us, honestly puzzled by our interest in a rotten novel the clubs had turned down so decisively.

But we were interrupted by Joe's secretary, who buzzed him to say that Harcourt Brace was on the phone.

"Excuse me," Joe said. "This call is really important."

Jack raised an eyebrow: what could be more important than a murder investigation? Only the next selection for Readers' Circle.

Joe's face broke into a grin and he let out a delighted whoop. "Yes, we heard. . . . The Book-of-the-Month judges went for the Japanese novel. We had it in, too. Our reader didn't have a clue. . . . Right. Only the judges and the Nobel Prize committee will ever understand it. . . . So where do we stand on the Civil War novel? You aren't going to let them hold it over for the next meeting, are you? A bird in the hand, after all . . . Our offer still stands. . . . Sure, of course. . . . And the Guild? . . . Right. You've got a deal. And we're delighted. Let's have lunch and celebrate. . . . Sure. It's my first selection, all on my own."

Joe had conveniently forgotten the existence of his Advisory Committee on Fiction. But he was right. It was *his* decision that counted.

He hung up, beaming. "It's ours. BOM wanted to hold it over for another month, but Harcourt wouldn't agree. And the Guild wanted it for a featured alternate, but they didn't come up with enough money. God, I'm relieved. Just wait here a minute while I tell the staff."

He disappeared, and I knew a party atmosphere was starting to build.

"It's really important to him, isn't it?" Jack said.

"Sure. Like solving a murder case to you. There won't be any work done around here for the next hour. Let's find the galleys on Dick's book—I know where they should be— and we'll clear out."

I doubt if Joe even missed us

9

Jack's apartment was in an old red-brick elevator building on a quiet, tree-lined street in Jackson Heights. His three rooms were as neat and as anonymous as a hotel suite, except for the books and records that lined one wall. I would have stopped to look at everything, but he was in a fever of impatience to get going on the cross-check between Marcia's novel and Dick's pornography.

It didn't take us long to prove that Jack was right.

Actually, Dick had done a fairly clever job. He had changed the characters' names and moved the location from Pennsylvania to Ohio, but otherwise he had simply copied out great chunks from Marcia's book.

"He was certainly true to his theory," I said. "He really *must* believe that all it takes to make a successful novel is to stir in a quantity of sex."

"But how could he have expected to get away with it?" Jack marveled.

"I don't know. Except he almost did. Who would ever really know except the author of the original, and maybe the editor? Suppose I had read Marcia's book ten years ago when it came out and then looked at this trash today. It would never occur to me to go back and look for a comparison. And remember: Marcia's book was a failure. It's not as if Dick was messing around with *Gone with the Wind* or *Pride and Prejudice.*"

"I still think he was taking an awful chance. And asking Marcia to read it—that was crazy."

"But why would he ever think that Mary Marcia Underwood was

142

Marcia Richardson? There's no picture on the jacket. There's not a clue on the flap copy to identify her as a New York editor. He didn't know that the Marcia he knew had ever written a novel. It was just sheer bad luck that made him stumble on her book to tamper with."

"I suppose so. I wonder how he found a copy. . . . Just poking around in the secondhand stores, maybe."

"It doesn't really explain about Elly, though," I said.

"No. Well, I'll phone Coleman, Kressman, and Yates to see how the investigation is proceeding. We'll have them hold our friend Mr. Frazier. He has a lot of explaining to do."

Jack had a rather involved discussion with Detective First Grade Sean Riordan, but all he passed on to me was that Dick Frazier had not been in the office that day; he had called in sick. Elly had done some typing for him on Monday, but that was apparently the extent of their contact. Dick had left the office at five o'clock as usual, and she had stayed behind to make some phone calls.

"We'll pick him up at his apartment," Jack said. "They're getting a warrant. I'll drop you off at home first before I meet Sean in the Village, on Charles Street."

"Don't drop me off at home. I want to see what happens."

"Don't be an idiot. The man is dangerous. *I* wouldn't walk in on him alone."

"Well, I should hope not. And I wouldn't either. Come on, Jack, at least let me find a coffee shop across the street. You'll never know I'm there. That's how I saw Ricardo, and that didn't do any harm."

"You're crazy. But I suppose if I don't drive you down there, you'll hop in a cab and show up anyway."

Actually, that hadn't occurred to me until he said it, but he was right.

"Let's take the book and the galleys with us." He looked around the apartment as if he had forgotten something. "I don't feel as if I've been much of a host," he said. "There's some great ice cream made with fresh raspberries in the freezer. . . ."

"Your mother was here again."

He laughed. "No, I had Sunday-night supper in Bayside and walked off with all the dessert. We'll have it later."

We were just emerging from the Queens Midtown Tunnel when

Jack solved the part of the puzzle that had really bothered him. "Now we know why Marcia's book was missing from her apartment," he said.

"We do?"

"Sure. She had pulled it out of the bookcase to check it against the galleys, and she had it there when Frazier came in. She challenged him with it."

"But why would he steal it afterward?"

"So that it wouldn't occur to anybody else to run a cross-check between the two books, of course."

"He could have put it right back in the bookcase."

"He could have. If he had wanted to go through the shelves and find a place for it. But I imagine he was in rather a hurry. . . . No, I know why he took it. There was blood on the book. He had to leave the galleys; it was only natural for her to have been reading them, as you and Joe have pointed out to me repeatedly. But to leave a blood-stained copy of her novel there, too? Even the dullest-witted detective would have wondered why she was comparing the two."

"I see." I tried to reconstruct the sequence of events. "Dick arrived on that Monday night, all unsuspecting, and there was Marcia confronting him with proof of plagiarism. . . ." I paused. "But she wouldn't have shot him for that."

"No. I suppose she was a little jittery, though, and just had the gun there for protection."

"And he spotted it and grabbed it. . . ."

"I don't suppose either of them was thinking very calmly."

"No. You get two authors' egos involved in a situation like that. . . . I think Dick Frazier must be more than slightly crazy," I said.

"I don't imagine that Marcia was the epitome of cool, collected wisdom under the circumstances, either. She was probably still shaken by the end of that affair with Ted Ferris, and then she found her half-forgotten novel had been turned into something pornographic."

We pulled into Charles Street, and Jack found a legitimate parking space for a change. He spotted the other detectives in an unmarked car half a block away. "You'll be all right, Karen? I don't know why

I said you could come. You're a distracting influence, do you know that?"

"I'll be quiet as a mouse. See, there's a sidewalk café with a perfect view. Give me something to read—I'll take Marcia's book—and I'll just pretend I never heard of you. Only, you be very careful."

"Always."

I strolled down the block and chose a table (at five P.M. on a weekday afternoon the place was less than half full), and I watched Jack enter the building across the street with two other detectives. The other man shot around to the back—to cover the rear exit, I suppose.

A lazy waiter finally showed up to take my order, and I tried dividing my attention between what was happening across the street (nothing) and Chapter One of *Changing Seasons: A Novel for Our Times* by Mary Marcia Underwood.

Fifteen boring minutes passed. What could be going on over there? Were they breaking down the door?"

And then I heard a voice behind me, faintly familiar, and chilling.

"Karen? It's Karen Lindstrom, isn't it?"

I turned around, and there was Dick Frazier, all by himself, standing at the entrance. He must have walked over from Eighth Street. It wasn't enough that he was a murderer—he was a liar, too, calling in sick at the office when there wasn't anything the matter with him at all.

I summoned up a weak smile, and he came over to my table.

"Waiting for somebody?" he asked

I nodded.

"Mind if I join you for a few minutes?"

I shook my head, still afraid to trust my voice.

"What brings you down to the Village?" Dick asked. "And so early, too. I didn't think the Berwyn Company let anybody out before six o'clock. To hear Nate talk, your noses are at the grindstone all the time."

"I'm meeting somebody," I said, frantically trying to pull a name out of the hat.

"From the office?" Dick asked. He seemed to have all the time in the world.

"No, not from the office." That would be dumb. We'd be in midtown and wouldn't come all the way down here. I had a sudden inspiration. "Meredith Baker," I said. "Know her?"

He shook his head.

I was relieved to find that out. "She's an agent," I resumed, with more confidence. "She lives down here. She was Marcia's agent," I babbled on idiotically. "We went to the funeral together in Philadelphia."

"Indeed." His eyes were very peculiar. Was he trying to check out what book I was reading? God, how would I ever explain that?

But he peered beyond me to call the waiter, and I slid Marcia's book off the table and into my lap. Dick didn't seem to notice, but I couldn't be sure. What was it Jack had said about the first two murders? "Both improvised. The man is quick-witted, whoever he is."

Jack, come back to me right now and I'll never get mixed up with anything like this again.

"You're drinking iced tea?" Dick asked.

I slid the glass closer to me, protectively, and agreed that it was, as he said, iced tea. Dick ordered a vodka and tonic, and I wondered how many of those he could drink before passing out. If we both just sat here indefinitely, what could happen?

I cast about frantically for an innocent topic of conversation, and my mind was an absolute blank.

"I was working at home," Dick volunteered. "It's easier to write copy away from the office, away from the phone calls. I haven't even had the radio on today."

Was that supposed to mean he was officially ignorant of Elly's death?

Aloud I said, "Are you working on the new RC campaign? What's it about?"

"I don't think I should tell you. Nate Meyer read me quite a lecture about talking out of turn. He wants all advertising information funneled through him."

"I see."

"He's quite a character, Nate. Rather violent at times, don't you think?"

I nodded cautiously.

"I just wondered what your detective friend thought of him."

"He doesn't like to talk to me about the case," I said, with considerable truth.

"But I'm sure you're very well informed about everything that's going on."

"I read the papers," I said shortly.

"Of course." He poured a little more tonic into his drink and stirred it thoughtfully.

I shifted away from him, and my book and my handbag both fell to the ground. In the scramble to pick things up—my pen had rolled into a crevice in the sidewalk and I never did recover my lipstick— Dick set Marcia's novel on the table between us. He flipped it open to the inscription, Marcia's brief note to her mother, and proceeded to read it.

"I brought it back from Philadelphia," I explained hastily. "Marcia's mother thought I might want to read her novel. I didn't know she had written a book."

"Do you like it?" Dick asked.

"I'm barely into the second chapter," I said. "I'll reserve judgment."

There was an uncomfortable pause.

"You work on MSI, don't you, Karen?"

"Yes."

"So you spend most of your time reading mystery and suspense stories."

"Yes."

"I just wondered if you read other manuscripts. More general books."

"Sometimes," I said cautiously. Like half the time, I thought, but I'm not going to admit to reading your book. I'm not even going to admit that I know you're Richmond Frazier, author. Plagiarizing author. Murdering author. But why Elly? Why in the world Elly?

"Do you believe in astrology, Karen?" Dick said, changing the subject abruptly.

"No. But then, I don't know much about it," I said diplomatically.

"A fascinating study," Dick said. "Though it does attract more than its share of kooks who misuse it."

"I suppose so."

"Your friend Elly Crawford thought she could solve this murder through astrology. I heard her talking to Lieutenant Morrison yesterday, asking for Marcia's birth date."

I nodded, chilled and fascinated at the same time. Why was he playing with dynamite this way?

"She seemed to think that Marcia's ex-husband was implicated," Dick went on.

"Everybody has a pet theory."

"I heard her trying to reach you yesterday, too."

"Yes, I was tied up at the time."

Dick finished his drink and signaled the waiter for another round. "Your friend must be very late," he said.

"Sometimes she doesn't have much conception of time." I looked at my watch—after 5:30. What was Jack doing? How long would those cops stay over there? And then I heard familiar footsteps and Jack was there, ten paces away on the sidewalk. Out of nowhere I was seized by inspiration. "Charley," I said, staring straight at Jack, who had paused to see who I was with. "Where in the world is Meredith? Charley is Meredith's husband," I explained to Dick—and incidentally to Jack, in case he had forgotten. "Charley, I want you to meet Dick Frazier. Dick, Charley Baker."

Jack came around the barrier, shook hands, and pulled a chair up to our table.

"I was just explaining to Dick," I raced on, "that I was supposed to meet Meredith here half an hour ago. What happened?"

"She's been delayed," Jack said calmly. "That's why she sent me along instead."

The waiter arrived with the second round of drinks, and Jack ordered a lemonade. The waiter scowled at him, but retreated. Then Jack reached across the table for the book and clumsily spilled my iced tea all over me, all over my new green and white striped dress that I'd only worn twice.

"What a shame, Karen," he said. "But if you go wash it out immediately, I think you can probably avoid a stain."

"We'll ask the waiter for some water," Dick said.

"No, no. I'll take care of it in the ladies' room." I clutched at my handbag and got away from there.

There was a pay phone in the back, right next to the ladies' room, and I searched frantically through my wallet for a dime. And then I hesitated. If I called the police emergency number, I'd have a long, confusing explanation to go through, and if they sent a squad car, Dick Frazier might see it and get away somehow.

So I checked out Dick's home phone number and dialed that. The voice on the other end was gruff and anonymous.

"Is this the police?" I whispered. "I mean, are you the detective in Dick Frazier's apartment?"

"What are you talking about? Who *is* this?"

"I'm calling for Lieutenant Morrison," I whispered a little louder. The waiter with Jack's lemonade paused to give me a fishy look, and I thought of tripping him, but decided against it. "I'm in the sidewalk café right across the street with Jack and Dick Frazier. Come over and help us."

"Lady, are you feeling all right? I can hardly hear what you're saying. What number are you calling?"

How could I remember what number I had called? "Frazier," I said a little louder. "Jack Morrison. Across the street in the sidewalk café. Look out the window if you don't believe me. *Hurry!*"

"Tell me again," the oaf on the other end was saying. "I think we got a bad connection."

Gritting my teeth, I went through it all again, slowly, my voice rising. I couldn't see Jack's table from where I was standing, and I was frantic. The waiter had not come back, either. "Across the street, you fool. Hurry!"

There was a small commotion on the sidewalk, out of range of my vision, and I left the receiver dangling and ran outside.

Dick Frazier was in handcuffs, between Jack and one of the detectives.

"Good work, Karen," Jack said. "I could have taken him myself, but I was glad to have Sean riding to the rescue. You must have been very convincing."

"No, I'm not the one you were talking to," the man named Sean explained. "Dave decided to keep you talking, in case it was some kind of trap. But I rushed over immediately."

149

"I see," I said shakily. "All of you with your little tricks all the time."

The other two detectives crossed the street to join us, but Jack didn't bother with introductions. "We have some work to do, Karen, and I'm afraid I'll have to abandon you here. Take a cab home. I'll see you there later."

Dick stood silent through all this, and they marched him off to one of the cars with no difficulty.

I stood in the little café, my dress still sopping with iced tea, the surly waiter at my elbow.

"I don't know what this is all about, lady," he said, "but somebody owes me for the drinks. That's five thirteen, including tax, plus twenty percent for sidewalk service, six twenty."

He was including the tax when he figured in the twenty-percent tip, but I didn't have the strength to fight him over the few pennies difference.

I went back to the ladies' room and dabbed at my dress, but the skirt would never be the same again. And I took a subway and a bus home. I had forgotten to get to the bank at noon, and the drinks had left me with exactly $1.63, plus two tokens.

Jack arrived a little after ten, hungry and elated and wrung out, all at the same time. I had cold chicken in the refrigerator, and I did something about a salad.

"Frazier confessed," Jack said, tucking in. "There were scratches on his arms where Elly had fought him off. We told him we would be able to match the scrapings with what we found under her fingernails."

"And can you?"

"I'm sure of it, as soon as the lab has run the tests."

"But how dumb of him to murder her at all."

"Yes. Well, I don't look for genius in most killers. It was pure fluke that it took us so long to arrest him for Marcia's death. There were too many other people around in the foreground."

"But why did he kill Elly? What happened?"

"He heard her on the phone," Jack explained, "saying she knew who the murderer was. At that point he didn't know what she meant.

So he followed her when she left the office, talked her into having dinner with him, at first decided to let her go because she was on the wrong track. As a matter of fact, he had almost brought her home and they were turning into Eighty-seventh Street when Elly suggested they go for a walk along the river."

"Yes, she liked to do that."

"Well, they were in the park, and the conversation got back to astrology again, signs and moons and cusps. Quite frankly, I got lost. I gather, though, that Elly found his planets even more peculiar than Harry Richardson's. They had discussed the murder earlier, at dinner, and I guess she found his curiosity suspicious. She had found out he was a writer, too, and somehow that made it worse. Anyway, she turned on him suddenly and accused him, said he had killed Marcia because she refused to buy his book for the Berwyn clubs. That wasn't quite accurate, of course, but it was near enough to the truth so that the police would start checking him out, and his book, too. Up to that point, remember, no cop had been near him."

"Yes, he must have thought he had gotten away with it completely."

"Right. So he pulled off his necktie and strangled her. He said he got the idea from some Hitchcock movie. Left the body in the bushes. And took the wallet to mislead us into thinking it was a simple mugging. He was obviously shaken up, though. That's why he didn't go in to the office today."

"And that crazy conversation with me . . ."

"He was running out of time and he knew it. And he thought he could pump you for information."

"Yes. Well, I'm glad that's all over. Elly's parents arrived this afternoon. Did you know that?"

"We talked to them. Mr. Crawford identified the body."

I shuddered. "Mrs. Crawford was here earlier this evening. With Eddy. She asked if there was anything of Elly's I wanted to remember her by. I couldn't think. They're staying overnight at a hotel and going back tomorrow with the body. Eddy is going, too."

"Yes. We finally located him. After that Zen lecture last night he went over to Fort Lee, to his uncle's restaurant. Spent the night with the family there."

151

"I see. It's all so ghastly. I keep thinking that if I had done something different, it wouldn't have happened. If I hadn't given Elly your phone number, if I had convinced her not to get mixed up in all of this . . ."

"Karen, that doesn't do any good. We can't go back and run it all through again. In the end, Elly had to be responsible for her actions; going off with Dick Frazier is something she did all by herself. It was tragic, a terrible mistake, but it was *her* mistake. We all make mistakes, all the time. Most of the time we survive them. It's unfair that Elly was killed for hers. But *life* is unfair, as one of our Presidents kept telling us."

He looked at me for some sign of agreement, but I didn't know what to say.

"In any case," Jack said, "I should have checked out Richmond Frazier right at the beginning."

"We told you over and over again that it was perfectly logical for Marcia to be reading that book. You can't blame yourself. . . ."

"That's what I mean. It's futile to go around carrying that kind of burden. The man with the real load of guilt in this case is Frazier. He consciously murdered two women, and he's been caught. I think there's enough evidence to convict him."

"Will you have to testify?"

"Probably. It all depends on how the district attorney chooses to present his case. But that's months in the future. We'll have gone through fifty other investigations by then. This will be behind us. You'll have read so much more mystery, suspense, and intrigue by then that I'll be positively dazzled by your erudition. I'll consult you on all my difficult cases."

"Will you really?"

"No, not really. Just the glamorous ones. Maybe once a year."

"But you'll tell me everything, so I don't worry about you?"

"Marriage is a privileged relationship. I'll know you can't testify against me."

He hadn't really answered my question, but I let it pass.

Jack looked around my apartment, and I knew we were both thinking the same thing. "After what happened," he said, "you won't want to stay here tonight."

152

"You're right."

"I know a place where you'll feel a lot safer."

"Yes."

"Safer from murderers, that is."

"Yes."

"I think you should pack a toothbrush and come home with me."

"Yes." I was beginning to wonder if I would ever disagree with him again.

"After all," he said, "we never did get around to sampling that ice cream."

I stopped dead in my tracks, and then I started to laugh.

We had the ice cream the next morning at breakfast. And that was good, too.